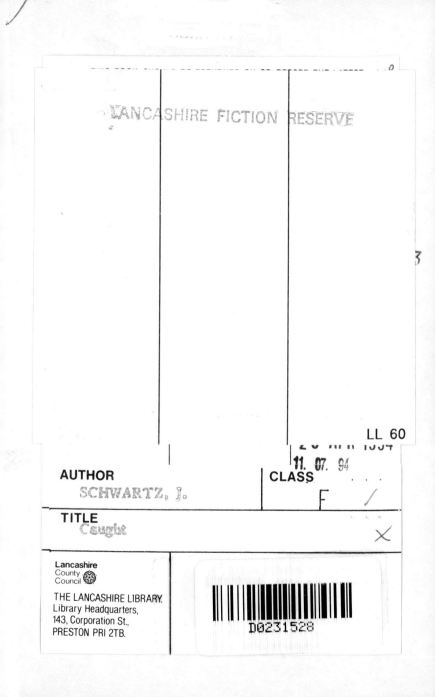

In this stunning first novel Jane Schwartz brilliantly captures the exhilarating world of rooftop pigeon-flying. Louie is still at school when she meets Casey. He is thirty-eight. It is their passion for pigeon-flying which brings them together and Casey breaks with the all-male tradition by asking Louie to become his apprentice. High above the grimy Brooklyn streets, far away from the constraints of school and family, Louie discovers a world of beauty, freedom — and violence. Here everything seems possible, including, for a while, an exceptional friendship. And here she learns from Casey the lesson every gambler has to learn — 'to be good, sometimes you have to lose'.

Jane Schwartz grew up in St Louis, Missouri, and now lives in Brooklyn, New York. She has lived in Afghanistan and India, among other places, and has worked as a journalist, puppeteer, waitress, sound recordist and teacher. She moved to North Brooklyn to research the background for this, her first novel, spending many hours on the rooftops of the city studying this unusual sport.

'Rich with the voice of the streets and with the most intimate details of being a child ... Moving, engrossing, thoroughly believable' — *New York Times Book Review*

'Impressive ... funny, fast-paced, but very serious in its concern with freedom and limitations' — *Maureen Howard*

Virago Upstarts is a new series of books for girls and young women. Upstarts are about love and romance, family and friends, work and school — and about new preoccupations — because in the last two decades the lives and expectations of girls have changed a lot. With fiction of all kinds — humour, mystery, love stories, science fiction, detective, thrillers — and nonfiction, this new series will show the funny, difficult, and exciting real lives and times of teenage girls in the 1980s. Lively, down-to-earth and entertaining, Virago's new list is an important new Upstart on the scene.

CAUGHT

Jane Schwartz

VIRAGO UPSTARTS

I would like to thank the real Brooklyn pigeon-flyers—
my teachers, my friends.

J.S.

Published by VIRAGO PRESS Limited 1987
41 William IV Street, London WC2N 4DB

First published in USA by Available Press, Ballantine Books, a division of
Random House Inc., New York, and simultaneously in Canada by Random
House of Canada Ltd, Toronto in 1985
Copyright © 1985 by Jane Schwartz

British Library Cataloguing in Publication Data

Schwartz, Jane   02883541
    Caught. — (Virago upstarts).
    I. Title
    813′.54 [F]   PZ7

    ISBN 0-86068-949-2

Printed in Great Britain by Cox & Wyman
Ltd. of Reading, Berkshire

for Buddy and Lorrayne

There are no classes in life for beginners; it is always the most difficult that is asked of one right away.

—RAINER MARIA RILKE
The Notebooks of Malte Laurids Brigge

1

THE ONLY REASON THEY LET ME GO UP ON THE ROOF WITH them that night was because I was so small. Neither my brother Frankie nor his best friend Michael Corsini could squeeze through the trap in the main coop, and they needed to get someone all the way inside if they were going to steal Bennie the Egg Man's pigeons. Bennie the Egg Man was a mutt. Every pigeon-flyer in Williamsburg knew that. He had cheated Frankie and Michael more than once, and for weeks they had been organizing their revenge.

Frankie's plan was simple. He would drop me into the inside feeding area and from there I would climb into the smaller coop, which didn't have a door on it. Then I would start grabbing the pigeons as fast as I could and passing them out to him and Michael, who would be waiting with burlap sacks. When I was finished, they would reach down and pull me back out through the trap. We would go up on a Friday because

1

Bennie played cards every Friday night while his wife went to bingo at St. Anthony's, up in Greenpoint. Everything was settled. Frankie asked me if I was afraid, and I said no.

But when Friday afternoon arrived, and the three of us were sitting cross-legged on the living room floor going over the plans a final time, Michael unexpectedly threatened to withdraw. He was worried, he said. He didn't want me to go. "She'll get scared, Frankie. She'll start crying or something." I started to protest, but Frankie signaled me to keep still. He let Michael ramble on and on until he ran out of steam. Then Frankie quietly reminded him about the punching bet, and Michael backed down. "Okay," he said, somewhat grudgingly. "I just hope she won't be sorry."

That was in October, 1958, when I was ten years old. So far, in spite of everything, I haven't been.

The punching bet was Frankie's idea, but I had endorsed it wholeheartedly. It had taken place the year before, when he bet each of his friends one dollar that they could hit me in the stomach as hard as they wanted and I wouldn't cry. I was five years younger than my brother and skinny as a stick. No one took him seriously except Michael. He showed up after dinner and refused to say hello to me. Frankie ushered us both out to the side alley where no one could see. He put a hand on my shoulder, and before I could straighten up Michael lunged forward and punched me just below the ribs. For a moment I couldn't breathe. I sucked in air, but couldn't swallow it. I was aware of Frankie's blurred features in front of my face and a voice that echoed from far away, asking if I was all right. When I heard that, I remembered. I blinked. I felt the tears well up behind my eyelids and I blinked harder, willing them to disappear. The next thing I knew, I heard the clatter of coins on the sidewalk. Frankie was congratulating me, tugging at my arm. I pulled away from him and stumbled upstairs to my room.

That was the first and only time we actually carried out the bet, but Frankie spread the word that even with his hardest punch, Michael Corsini hadn't been able to make me cry. Within a few days my reputation was made. After that, Michael even said I could go up on his roof with them. They wouldn't let me be partners, though; they said I was too young and didn't know enough about the pigeons. That was okay with me. I liked the birds and I liked to watch them fly, but in the beginning, the main reason I followed them up there was just because I wanted to go everywhere they went and do everything they did. In fact, for a long time, what I really wanted was just to *be* them.

It had been dark for hours when we finally left our house and headed for Bennie's. The three of us marched in silence all the way down Lorimer until we reached Metropolitan Avenue. Then, staring straight ahead, Michael said, "You sure you ain't scared?"

"I'm sure," I said.

"Aw, you're just too dumb to be scared." But he smiled, and there was no meanness in his voice.

I pulled my cap down as far as I could on my forehead. My hair was short and stuck out only a little at the back and sides. I glanced up at Frankie as we waited for the light. He was fairer than I, and because his hair was cropped close to his head it appeared even lighter than its natural chestnut shade. He had serious green eyes and a constellation of freckles across his cheeks. Everything else about him was straight lines: narrow, even eyebrows; a smooth nose; a slit for a mouth. How I wanted to look like Frankie in those days! I could do nothing about my dark hair and even darker eyes, so brown the irises disappeared. But one summer, determined to have his freckles, I had taken a pencil and stabbed my face repeatedly until the point broke off in my cheek.

We walked on. Just before we reached Bennie's, Frankie stopped abruptly. "Hey, Louie, wait up." He leaned over and tugged at the zipper of my jacket. It was already zipped as high as it could go. I wanted to tell him not to worry, but he immediately turned away.

"Okay, you guys. Let's go!"

We hurried up the stoop to Bennie's house. Everything depended on the outside door. If it was locked, we'd have to scrap the plan until the next week. If it was open, we'd be home free. There were lights on in the second-floor apartment, but if we kept quiet they'd never hear us on the roof. Bennie lived above these people, on the top floor. Michael turned the knob. The door gave way easily and he walked in. Frankie touched me on the shoulder and I went next. My heart was thumping, but as long as Frankie was nearby I had no reason to be afraid.

Enough light filtered up from the downstairs hall so that we could see all the way up, but none of us needed it. Stairs were stairs, and when we got to the third floor they would stop.

"Okay," Michael whispered. In front of us was a thin iron ladder that ran straight up from the hallway to a wooden hatch in the roof. There was a hasp on it, but no one had bothered to lock it. Sometimes people got careless when they had their coops directly above their own apartments. They figured they'd be sure to hear if anything was going on. Maybe Bennie was too smart for his own good, I thought. That was one of my mother's favorite expressions, and I repeated it to myself as I climbed through the hatch.

When we stepped outside onto the roof, it was like entering another world. The night sky stretched out over us, pierced by a million stars; their glitter made the darkness seem alive. I ran over to the edge to get a view of the city.

"Hey!" Frankie hissed at me. "Get over here and get down! And keep quiet!"

"I'm sorry," I whispered.

"This ain't a game!"

"I said I'm sorry!"

"Okay, okay."

Michael had already jumped onto the lower part of the roof of the pigeon coop. There were two levels, separated by a narrow trap that opened inward. Frankie made a stirrup with his hands and boosted me up to the top. Michael was pulling the burlap bag out from under his windbreaker.

"Come on, come on," he urged.

I scrambled up and sat still for a second, listening to the birds. Aware of us, they had started flapping their wings and fluttering down from the boxes where they perched. I could hear the thin whine of air passing through their feathers as they scattered across the coop, darting from ledge to ledge. When they were peaceful, their cooing was soft and bubbly, like when you blew through a straw in your milk. Now they took up a deep *whoooo-whooooo*ing that rippled out in wave after wave. I knew they would take off when I crashed into the coop. Pigeons were skittish by nature, but they weren't dangerous. They'd

5

never even try to peck at you unless you were practically torturing them.

Frankie climbed up behind me. "Okay," he said. "Let's go."

I had to lie down on my stomach to squeeze through. Frankie pulled the wire to open the trap, then pushed my hips through while Michael held on to my arms. When my legs fell free into the space below, there was another flurry from the pigeons. I hung there for a moment, bent over at the waist, the movable door of the trap resting against my lower back. I was pretty sure I could force my shoulders through, but I was beginning to worry about my head. As Michael lowered me into the coop, the tarpaper grated across my chest. Finally I was suspended from my armpits, ready to drop as soon as my head pushed through.

"Take off your cap," Frankie commanded, pulling it from my head. "Now turn your face to the side."

"Be careful," I warned.

"Look," Michael answered, "I'm doing the best I can."

I slipped my head through. Michael let go of my arms a fraction of a second too soon, and even though I was only about a foot off the ground, I crashed down with a loud *thunk!* I lost my balance and fell on my side. We froze, terrified that the noise would alert the neighbors. When nothing happened, Frankie stuck his face into the trap. "Okay, quick! Get going!"

"Gimme my hat!"

"Here!" He threw it at me. "Now move!"

There was no door to the inside coop, just a rectangular hole about three feet high, starting a foot off the ground. I hunched over and stepped inside, cradling my face in the crook of my arm to protect it from the rush of birds. I kept still for a minute, waiting for them to calm down enough so that the feathers stopped flying and most of them had settled back onto their perches. Then I went after them.

Catching a pigeon is like swatting a fly: you just have to get close enough so that the warning swish of air doesn't hit them till it's too late to escape. I couldn't hold them with one hand like the boys could because my hands were too small. Usually you gripped them under the belly, pinning their feet between your middle fingers while you pressed their wings down with your thumb. Since I couldn't span their bodies like that, I had to pin them against the wall or the roost one at a time and then stick them under my arm. I worked quickly. I could tuck two under my left arm while I caught a third; then I'd have to stumble out of the hole and hand them through the trap to Frankie and Michael. Although it was dark inside the coop, my eyes adjusted pretty quickly. There was a bulb, of course, but we couldn't risk anyone seeing the light.

I had finished seven or eight rounds when I heard a bang. I dropped the red teaguer I was holding and raced over to the trap.

"Frankie!" It was the loudest whisper I could manage. "Frankie, what's wrong? What's going on?"

"He'll kill us!" Michael hissed. "What's the matter with you?" He jumped down from the coop. "Come on, willya? I swear he won't hurt her, she's a *girl*. Come *on*, damn it!"

From my position inside the coop, all I could see was a narrow strip of sky. I stretched my fingertips up through the opening and waved them in the dark.

"Frankie!" It was the only time I called out loud. Nobody answered. I heard people running back and forth, then Michael cried, "The fire escape!" and someone screamed, "I'll get you motherfucking thieves!" I ducked back into the coop and cowered in the far corner, my knees pulled up tight against my chest, my eyes riveted on the door. Frankie had assured

7

me that the plan was foolproof. It never occurred to me that he could have been wrong. My legs were dissolving with fear; even if I got the chance, I wouldn't be able to run. I knew that if Frankie didn't come back and get me, someone else would.

The pigeons, a few at a time, were still circling the small room. I listened to the *whirrrr, whirrrr* of their wings. The coop was close and musty; my breath began coming in shallow gasps. Gradually the pigeons settled down again and the silence from outside began to fill the coop. It was this silence that convinced me I was trapped. Even if everyone had left the roof, there was no way I could escape on my own. All I could do was wait.

I told myself that Frankie would come back and everything would be okay. I repeated this over and over, willing myself to believe it, when suddenly something in the air changed. I didn't hear anything, but I sensed the difference right away. The birds straightened up, their cooing got louder, their trills deeper and faster. My throat was dry and tight, as if I were gagging on feathers. I couldn't stop shaking. Then I heard the grating sound of metal against metal. The door to the coop banged open and the light snapped on. In that instant, I glimpsed the red face of a huge, potbellied man. He stuffed his frame through the opening and spotted me right away. "You motherfucking son of a bitch!" He charged across the coop and the pigeons exploded. They crashed wildly back and forth across his path until the air was thick with wings and feathers and dust. He staggered through this onslaught straight to my corner.

"You rotten little thief!" He whacked me across the back, then grabbed my arm so hard he almost pulled it out of the socket. "Nobody steals *my* birds!" He jerked me to my feet, but turned so quickly I lost my balance. He dragged me behind him over the wooden divider, out of the coop, and over to the edge of the roof without saying a word. Then he released my arm for a split second, only to grab both my heels and suddenly haul me up into the air. The world rushed by in a blur. My cap flew off as he whipped me through the air, over the railing, and swung me upside down off the edge of the roof. I stiffened and churned my arms against the emptiness. The pale green shingles of the house, only a foot away, seemed as distant as the stars. I reached for them, desperate to feel something solid. I struggled to straighten up, but all I could manage was a grotesque twitching from my waist. I knew not to look down, to focus only on the side of the house. If only I could touch it, I thought, I would be okay. I tried again, but my arms couldn't reach that far. They couldn't reach anything. That was the scariest feeling of all—until he let go of one leg. I screamed; or rather, I tried to scream. All that came out was a harsh, retching noise that caught in my throat.

"So ya like birds, huh?" He grunted a short, dry laugh. "So fly home, ya goddamn two-bit pigeon thief!" He whooshed me straight up in the air and back over the roof. My stomach fell out like it does when you come down fast from a high swing, and I collapsed at his feet.

"Next time I'm droppin' ya straight down over the side, understand?"

I didn't say anything.

"Who brought ya up here?"

I curled into a ball and inched away from him.

"Okay, don't talk. We're goin' down by the pet store and show everybody what a pigeon thief looks like."

He pinned me against his body with one huge arm so that I

was parallel to the ground, facing away from him. I tried kicking out a few times but my legs were so weak I could hardly move them. He squeezed us both through the hatch and down the ladder. On the street, people glanced over at us, but no one made a move to interfere. I swore to myself that I wouldn't cry out for help. He carried me like that all the way over to the corner of Roebling and South First, where he pushed open the door to Joey's Pigeon Shop with one foot, burst into a roomful of men, and dumped me on the floor. The air was heavy with smoke. I scrambled to my feet and glared at him.

"Ya see this kid?" he announced. "This here's the latest thing in pigeon thieves."

Several men looked up from the round table in the back where they were playing cards. I noticed one man in particular: he was perched on a metal stool just behind the cardplayers, and he had coppery red hair and a thick beard. I had never known anyone with a beard before.

"I just found him in the coop. His buddies took off down the fire escape."

"He-ey, looks like the big time, Bennie." A couple of guys laughed.

"Yeah, well, what do *you* do when *you're* bein' tapped off?"

"Aw, now just take it easy, Bennie, take it easy." A short man in a faded sweater was leaning over the glass counter in front of the feed bins. He had messy grey hair and the cloudy eyes of an old dog. One of his front teeth was missing.

"Well, what do *you* think I should do with him, Joey? They made off with my birds."

"You'll get your birds back, don't worry." Joey remained calm. "You know who took them?"

10

"That kid Michael, I think. You know, kid used to chase for me?"

Joey nodded. "So whyn't you go over there and see his old man?"

"Cause I wanna know who *he* is first." He poked me in the arm and I jerked away. "You seen him in the shop before?"

Joey tapped out a cigarette from a pack of Camels and struck a match. The red-haired man caught his eye and grinned. Joey looked like he was trying not to smile. "Nope," he said. "Never been in here before."

"Come over here." I knew the red-haired man was talking to me, but I bent down to tie my shoe. "Come *over* here." His voice was serious, not mean; still, for some reason, I hesitated.

"Here." Bennie pushed me towards him. I shook off his hand and walked over on my own.

For a moment, the redheaded man just looked at me.

"You can have him," Bennie muttered.

"*Her*," the red-haired man corrected. He reached his hand out slowly and touched my face. "Ain't that right, sweetheart?"

"What are you, *nuts*?" Bennie squawked.

Everyone started to laugh.

"Hoo, Bennie, you must be losin' your touch, can't even tell the difference no more!"

"Maybe that's why your hens ain't been layin' eggs, Bennie!"

"I knew you was *old*, Bennie, but not *that* old!"

"Aw, shut up!" Bennie snatched me roughly by the shoulder. I don't know what came over me. Maybe I was just startled, or maybe I had been yanked around one too many times. Maybe I sensed that I had found some measure of protection in that room. At any rate, when Bennie grabbed me, I twisted my neck around and spit directly into his face.

11

Everybody froze. I glanced instinctively at the door. A figure had appeared out of nowhere, breathless, poised to come in—and clearly blocking my exit. I didn't know whether to feel terrified or relieved. It was my mother.

"What's going on here?" Her voice was dangerously low. Even Bennie moved out of her way. She walked deliberately across the shop and smacked me in the face so hard I fell against the glass counter.

"Ma!" I cried. My mouth filled up with a salty taste and I slid down between the stacks of fifty-pound feed bags.

"Don't you *ever* spit at anyone again, you hear me? What were you doing stealing pigeons? Michael's father called and said—"

"Where's Frankie?" I broke in. As soon as I said his name, my chin started to quiver.

"What do you care where's Frankie? Frankie got you into this mess in the first place."

The room blurred. I blinked faster and faster but the tears had already started to escape. I bit down on my thumb, hard enough to break the skin, but even that didn't help. A horrible wheezing sound burst out of my mouth, and suddenly I was crying in the high, ragged sobs of a small child. I tried to hide, to bury myself behind the stiff paper feed sacks. After a moment, my mother put her arms around me and pulled me to my feet. "Come on," she said softly. "Come on, now. That's enough."

I pressed my face against her stomach so no one could see me cry. Joey came around from the counter and held the door open. He patted my head awkwardly as we went out.

"Hey, what about my birds?" Bennie whined after us.

There was a second of dead silence.

"Aw, shut the fuck up," someone muttered from the back of the room. And then, embarrassed, " 'Scuse me."

Although the words were a shock, I knew immediately who had said them. I didn't even have to look up, because the voice had already become familiar to me. It belonged to the red-haired man.

2

AFTER WE CROSSED METROPOLITAN AVENUE, I
wriggled out from under my mother's arm and hurried ahead,
wiping my nose on the sleeve of my windbreaker. When she
caught up to me at the streetlight, she put her hand on my
shoulder; I tried to shrug her off again, but this time she
tightened her grip and forced me to face her.

"Louie, are you sure you're okay?"

"I'm fine."

She let go, and I walked on.

The streets were deserted that time of night, but up ahead an
irregular stream of headlights punctuated the darkness as cars
whizzed by on the expressway. Beyond the overpass, the sky
seemed to have faded. Earlier, when we climbed out onto
Bennie's roof, it had been deeper and more intense; bright with
the scattered stars but still impenetrable. From the street, I
noticed that the night wasn't really black at all, but more like a
wash of watercolor blue, thin and diluted.

I slowed down so my mother wouldn't have to walk so fast, but still stayed a few steps ahead. "Is Junior at the store?" I asked. We were almost home.

She nodded.

Junior Mara was our stepfather. When Ma had married him, less than a year before, Frankie and I had already known him most of our lives. He owned the grocery store on Nassau Avenue and had been giving us free candy for years. I used to find excuses to stop by his store after school. I loved licorice, and he would always slip me a Switzer's bar or a package of Blackjack gum on my way out. When he was just the grocer, I liked him well enough, but after he started dating my mother things changed, and I never took anything free from him again.

A crack of light showed under Frankie's door. Ma hung up her coat and called to him from the kitchen. The three of us took our regular seats around the white Formica table. No matter what happened, whether we were eating dinner or doing homework or just sitting there talking, we always gravitated to the same spots around the table; without its ever having been stated as a rule, a kind of territorial inviolability had been established in our household. Even in the midst of turmoil, we sank automatically into "our" seats.

I propped my elbows on the table and observed Frankie, who refused to meet my eyes. Ma immediately got up and fixed herself a cup of tea while we waited in silence. When she returned to her place, she demanded once again to know exactly what had happened.

"Nothing." I rubbed the dirt from my palms into thin black snakes and dropped them on the table.

She ignored me. "Frankie?"

"Ma, I told you already. You know about Bennie the Egg

15

Man. He cheated Michael out of some birds, from before. It's not fair, Ma. He cheats everybody."

"And that makes it okay to steal?"

"Well, Ma, it's not really stealing. I mean, he probably stole half the birds up there anyway."

"I don't care what he does. Louie, did you know what they were doing? Did you go up there to steal those birds?"

"He cheated Michael."

She took a sip of the steaming tea. Under the glare of the kitchen light, the lines in her face had deepened. When she set the cup down, her tea sloshed over into the saucer. "I'm ashamed of you both. That's all I have to say. Especially you, Frankie. I can't be home all the time, I've got to work, and you're supposed to set an example around here. I expect you to take better care of your sister than this."

"Ma! He doesn't have to take care of me! I'm not a baby. I can take care of myself."

"Is that so?" Her mouth was set in a hard line. "You certainly did a fine job tonight, Louie. Do you know what they could have done to you? They throw thieves off the roofs around here. You wouldn't have been the first."

Frankie pushed back his chair and took a step towards the refrigerator.

"Sit down here!"

"Ma, I just want some milk."

"I said sit down!"

Frankie and I stared at the table. Ma finished her tea in quick, uncharacteristic gulps. When she spoke again her voice was softer, but tightly controlled.

"You remember Russ O'Neal? He used to go fishing with your father? Maybe you're too young, Louie." She reached for my hand but I clenched my fingers into a tight little fist.

"I remember," I lied. I couldn't stand to admit that there was anything about my father I didn't know.

"Russell used to fly pigeons—everyone around here used to have birds, you have no idea, you kids didn't invent the game—and one night Russell caught someone trying to break into his coop. So you know what he did? He grabbed the man and threw him off the roof. Just like that." She stood up, hesitated, then took her cup over to the sink and rinsed it out. She raised her voice so we could hear above the running water. "Only he turned out to be a kid, thirteen years old. Big for his age, but still a kid. He was in the hospital for months, but he lived. There were no witnesses, and Russell knew a few people, so that was that." She dried her hands and hung the towel on the rack. I thought she was going to say something else, but she didn't. She just stood there with her back to us, smoothing wrinkles from the towel.

After a while, Frankie looked up. "Ma," he said. "I'm sorry we caused all this trouble. We won't do it again. I promise."

I nodded in agreement.

"I'm sure you won't, because from now on I don't want either one of you fooling around with those pigeons under any circumstances. Not here, not at Michael's, not anywhere."

"Ma!" Frankie and I cried out with one voice.

"I mean it. There's nothing to discuss."

"But Ma, that's not fair!"

"What you did wasn't fair either. Junior said it from the beginning, and I should have listened to him then. Stay away from the birds and for the time being, stay away from each other. And don't ever—*ever*—let me hear of you stealing anything ever again."

Frankie and I exchanged looks. I started to plead our case,

17

but a change took place in my mother's expression that was so unsettling I forgot to speak. Her features shifted and hardened, like water freezing into ice. In one instant, something alive and fluid ceased to exist, and in its place was an obstacle so icy and immovable that I instinctively knew better than to shatter myself against its edges.

Without another word, Frankie and I got up from the table and went to our rooms. Ma didn't move; she didn't kiss us, she didn't even say good night.

I pulled back the curtain to my alcove and wished once again that I could have a real door. I didn't mind that my room was small, and most of the time I didn't mind that it was off the living room instead of at the back, like the two real bedrooms. I only wished I had a door, something solid that I could shut. I longed for the finality of a lock clicking into place. I had asked Junior to build me one for Christmas, and swore I wouldn't want any other presents, but he said it would be easier to buy a house with another bedroom, and how would I like that? I told him I didn't want another bedroom, just a door.

I sat down at my desk and touched the framed photograph of my father. I had lots of pictures of Poppy, but this one was my favorite. In it, he was holding a cat he had just rescued from a burning apartment in Queens. They're both looking out at the camera, cheek to cheek, and the cat has one paw around my father's neck. My father is smiling. On his helmet, you can read the numbers of his firehouse—Ladder Company 110. Three months later my father was dead. I was seven years old.

The funeral didn't have any connection to Poppy, in spite of the hundreds of firemen who were present. Their white gloves made them look strange. People spoke to me, but I didn't know what to say back. Frankie held my hand all morning, and for once I didn't object. Afterwards, it was Frankie, not my mother, who explained to me over and over what had happened, how Poppy and two other firemen had gone back inside the paint factory to search for missing workers when, without warning, the roof gave way and collapsed.

"Louie?"

I jerked my hand away from the photograph. Frankie had pulled the curtain back just enough to stick his head through.

"What do you want?"

"I just want to say I'm sorry, Louie. I'm sorry things got messed up. Honest."

"Ma slapped me in the face, Frankie."

His eyes widened. "She did?" Frankie didn't impress easily, so that made me feel better. "You okay?"

I nodded.

"Sure?"

"Yeah. I'm sure. Frankie?"

"Yeah?"

"Oh. Never mind."

"What?"

"Nothing. Never mind. Really."

"Okay. Well, good night."

"'Night."

I got up and started to undress. My arm was sore where Bennie's fingers had clamped on to me. The pain reminded me of his roof; it seemed like it had all happened a long time ago. When I started to recall the night's events, I was surprised by the number of details I had absorbed. I could

19

replay everything in my mind just as it had taken place. The
sandpaper-roughness of the shingles burned with such vividness
before my eyes that I might have been staring at a movie.
Then, as I slid my jeans off, I discovered another, much more
serious bruise that I hadn't even been aware of. A discolored
mound of flesh had risen over my left thigh. It was yellow at
the edges, melting to pale green and then bright, throbbing
purple and red violet. I hadn't felt a thing, just a slight stiffness
as we walked home. I examined the injury with a mixture of
horror and awe. This was where my leg had hit the wooden
divider as Bennie hauled me out of the coop. I must have been
numb with terror not to have felt such a blow. I touched it
lightly, then pressed harder and harder till it sent a jolt of pain
straight up my spine. The center was hot and swollen, and I
could detect a hard knot underneath. When I tried to bend
my knee, the stiffness made my entire leg ache. The bruise had
spread out like a stain against the paleness of my skin, starting
just below the circle of my underpants and reaching halfway to
my knee. I finished stepping out of my jeans and left them
lying on the floor.

The bottom drawer of the dresser creaked as I opened it and
pulled out my red-and-white pajama top. My leg was too sore
for the bottoms; besides, I didn't want to cover it up. Even as I
crawled under the covers, the slight weight of the blanket
crushed upon the bruise, setting off a white-hot burning beneath
the surface of my skin. I flicked off the light, not because I
was tired, but because in the absence of a door the darkness
offered some separation from the outside. I didn't want Junior
coming in and asking questions when he got home.

I rearranged the covers to form a little pocket of air around
my thigh. I had been knocked and scraped and punched

before, but I had never had a wound like this. I couldn't leave it alone. My fingers kept creeping back to it, stroking it, caressing it, pressing it lightly, just hard enough to accentuate the steady ache it produced on its own—then pressing down harder ... harder ... harder ... I could make it hurt so much it almost stopped hurting. I covered it gently with my palm, and the hot throbbing continued. I lay like that for a long time, staring into the darkness, my fingers unable to ignore the pain. And long before I dropped off to sleep, as I kept slowly circling the bruise, just barely grazing it with my fingertips, I realized that I was not thinking of Bennie, who after all had caused it, but of the strange man with the beard and the low voice, the man in the pet shop who had called me "sweetheart" and touched my face with the back of his hand.

3

ABOUT A WEEK LATER, WALKING HOME FROM SCHOOL,
I got the distinct impression that someone was following me. I
looked over my shoulder several times, but the sidewalk was
empty. It wasn't until a man's voice called out, "Hey, sweetheart!" that I noticed the battered green station wagon
cruising slowly along beside me. Thinking the driver had made
a mistake, I ignored him. When he called a second time, I
stopped. I don't know why I didn't recognize him immediately.
He was grinning right at me, and the beard was unmistakable.

"What's the matter, you scared of me or something?" He
removed his faded tweed cap and ran his hand through his
hair. His knuckles were raw and cracked, even though it was
still October and hadn't really begun to turn cold.

I shook my head.

"Then come over here." He tapped the passenger door. I
moved a step closer. On the seat beside him was an open

bottle of wine. He saw me look at it and screwed the cap back on. "So." He looked at me. "What's new, babe?"

I shrugged. I tried to think of something to say, but I didn't know if he meant what was new in general, or with me, or with the pigeons. I took so long trying to decide what to say that I began worrying he might think I was stupid.

"You know who I am?"

I nodded. "From the pigeon store."

"Very good. The girl can talk. Now tell me something, are you a real pigeon-flyer or just a thief?"

It took a moment for the words to register. When they did, I was so stunned that I clasped my books against my chest and stalked off.

He got stuck at the light but managed to catch up to me a block later. "Hey, what's the matter with you? Can't you even take a joke?"

I turned.

"You gotta have thicker skin than that if you want to fly in this neighborhood. Don't be sore." He leaned across the seat, unlocked the passenger's side, and pushed open the door. "The reason I asked is, I need some help up on the roof and I thought of you. I thought you might be interested."

My heart skidded to a halt. He needed help up on his roof? He had thought of *me*? His timing couldn't have been worse. I wasn't supposed to fly pigeons any more. I wasn't supposed to be talking to strangers either, for that matter— especially men. Especially men with the syrupy smell of wine on their breath. And I certainly wasn't supposed to go up on their roofs.

"So what do you want to do? You want to come up or not?"

I hesitated. Silently, I rehearsed my refusal. No. No, thank

you. I'd like to, but— My mother says— I'm not allowed—
No. Then I took a deep breath and said yes.

"Well come on then," he said. "Get in. We ain't got much
time."

"Where's the roof? Maybe I could just walk over and meet
you there. I like to walk."

"Get in the car! I ain't gonna do nothing. Jesus Christ."

I got in and huddled near the door, placing my books
between me and the man with the beard. His hair wasn't
nearly as red as I remembered, but it shone in the afternoon
light. Up close, I noticed his eyes for the first time. They were
pale blue, almost as colorless as glass. I still didn't know his
name.

"You coming from school?" He made a U-turn away from
Metropolitan.

I nodded.

"You like school I bet, huh?"

"No."

"No? I thought girls your age always liked school. What's the
matter with you?"

I didn't know what to say. I supposed something was the
matter with me, but I didn't have a name for it.

"You don't talk much, do you?"

"Yes, I do!" The protest was automatic. I did talk. At least, I
always had in the past, but he unsettled me; I couldn't explain
it. No matter what I said, my answers never seemed to match
his questions. We rode the rest of the way in silence, and I
was beginning to wonder where he was taking me when he
pulled up to the corner of Bedford and North Eighth. I
jumped out of the car and stared up at the red brick factory that
dominated the block. I heard him get out and lock his door.

"You're *Casey*?"

His lips curved into a half smile that he tried to suppress.
"Yeah. How'd you know?"

I turned back to the roof. Even from the curb I could see the
edge of a huge steel coop that ran almost thirty feet across.
"Michael Corsini told me about you. You had the birds on
Myrtle Avenue, right?"

Casey laughed. "That's right. Best flying stock you ever saw.
Unbelievable. I ain't never seen pigeons like that. They used to
dive-bomb the other stocks, I swear to god, like they was going
after them on purpose. Then they'd butterfly right out of the
turn and come up with strays every time. Every time, man, I
couldn't believe it. They flew like they was one bird, they was
so tight. These turkeys I got now, they ain't bad, don't get me
wrong, but those birds on Myrtle Avenue was something else.
And the funny thing was, everybody used to want to know
what I did to them, how I got them to fly like that, but I
didn't do nothing, man, that was just the way they was."

He headed for the open door of the old building. There was a
painted sign outside that read "Reliable Fabricators." I
followed him into the entryway, which was littered with candy
wrappers, order forms on pink and yellow paper, and empty
Coke bottles.

"This place is a dump," Casey said. "Don't pay no attention.
We just use the roof." He was already panting when we
reached the third floor, and by the time we'd gotten to the sixth
I was out of breath as well. We stopped on the landing for a
minute. On each side of the hallway there was a door. One said
"Solomon's Button Manufacturers" on a metal plaque, and the
other had the word "DOAK" painted right on the door itself. I
could hear a dog barking inside. Both doors had three or four
locks on them.

25

Casey put his hand on the railing and started up the last flight. "What's your name, by the way, if you don't mind my asking?"

"Louie." I hesitated, unsure if I was supposed to say my last name or not. While I was deciding, he went on.

"How'd you know about Myrtle Avenue?" He pulled out a huge key ring. "That musta been fifteen years ago. You weren't even born."

"I know, but my brother and Michael Corsini are friends, and Michael knew about you from his father, who used to fly birds. He said everybody knows you. We fly—we used to fly—by Michael's house, over on Ainslie Street, by the Italian restaurant. You know where I mean?"

"Yeah? That was you? You got about three birds, right?" His dimples cut deep into his cheeks and disappeared under his beard.

"Very funny."

"Well, am I right or wrong? Tell me how many birds you got."

"We had thirty-four Flights—and they were good, too."

"Hey, the big time." He unbolted the door. "I'm gonna show you *birds*. You ready for this?" He leaned his shoulder into the heavy steel door and pushed.

I hadn't noticed how dark the stairwell was until the door burst open and the brightness of the roof swallowed up everything. For an instant, I was blinded. I stepped into the center of the roof, feeling slightly unreal. This was nothing like being on the fire escape, or even up on Bennie's. This was the tallest building in the neighborhood. There was nothing but space in every direction. It was like being on top of the world. Around the perimeter of the entire roof ran a retaining

wall about three and a half feet high. I walked over and looked
out. From this vantage point I could see everything from the
tiny figure pushing a shopping cart two blocks away to the three
bridges that spanned the lower East River, joining Brooklyn to
Manhattan. From the back of the roof the entire Manhattan
skyline stretched along the horizon. I could see down onto
rooftops in all directions. The tinier they seemed, the bigger I
felt.

"Come here," Casey hollered from inside the screened-in area
that separated the two sections of the steel coop. "I want to
show you the setup."

I turned and ran over to him. Frankie was not going to
believe this.

"This here's the main coop." He unlocked one side and
hundreds of birds whirred into action, crowding past one
another as they fluttered into the screened area. Their cooing
got louder and more excited as Casey flicked open the outer
screen door and let them stream onto the roof. "We'll just let
'em out for a little while. I can't really stay up here right now.
Come on. Take a look inside." The deserted coop was dark,
with only a small window at each end. The air was so thick
with dust it made my nose tighten, but the smell was not
unpleasant. It was warm and sort of doughy, but the boxes
that lined all four walls were caked with droppings that looked
as if they had been accumulating for months. The floor was
carpeted with them. Feathers drifted through the air and
collected in the corners, stuck to the excrement.

"This is all the babies from the spring and summer. They're
pretty much mixed in with the main stock now, but we kept
the rest of the flying birds in the other side, them that we didn't
want mated up."

I followed him back outside onto the roof. He put his fingers in his mouth and whistled once, a long, piercing sound. The pigeons took off.

"I ain't even gonna chase 'em today. I just want them to move their butts and get a little exercise."

At the far end of the coop was a low metal tray filled with water. Casey dumped it out, disappeared behind the low kiosk in the center of the roof that housed the chimney, and emerged with a hose trickling water.

"The pressure ain't always too great up here, but don't worry, it comes up eventually. That's the shanty. I got a 'lectric heater up there for the winter. You can freeze your— I mean, you can really freeze up here during the winter. But you can always go in there. I got a hot plate you can make soup or something. Go take a look."

Inside the shanty was a steel trunk that held three fifty-pound sacks of corn. On an open shelf above it were a pair of binoculars and rusted Maxwell House cans filled with plastic color-bands. Outside the door, two hooples hung on metal hooks alongside a red flag. The shanty had large windows on three sides and an ill-fitting door that could be latched from either side. A bench was built in against the length of the back wall, covered with a ratty green sofa cushion and an army blanket wadded up like a pillow at one end. Under the bench there was a copy of a magazine called *American Pigeon Journal*. Casey poked his head in.

"This is all yours?" I asked.

He smiled. "Well, the roof ain't. I just rent the roof. But everything else on it is. I built all this myself. The coop, the shanty, everything. Not bad, huh?"

"It's beautiful!"

"It ain't bad. A guy named Fingers helped out, that was my partner from before, but he split a while ago. We were up here three years together, then he backed out. What the hell. It's all mine now. You're better off alone anyway, you don't never gotta have no headaches with nobody, right?"

I nodded, but only because I could see he wanted me to. I had liked flying with Michael and Frankie, but maybe he and his partner hadn't gotten along. He put his hand on my shoulder and steered me out of the shanty and over to the wooden steps that ran along the front of the coop.

"Sit down. Now, here's what I want." He spoke as if I'd been coming up there for years. "What time you get out of school?"

"Two-forty-five. Why?"

"Okay, that's good. What you can do, if you wanna chase for me, is start coming in after school and just letting 'em out. I'll get up around four, four-thirty, after I get out of work, and I'll spend a couple of weeks getting you used to everything. They're in good shape. The older ones is all finished moulting now and they're getting strong again. You can let them out and start chasing them. What I'd like before long is to have you come up before school just to feed 'em—especially in the winter. They can't go all day without food when it's cold, and sometimes I can't get here before work."

I was dazed. He was talking as if we had already made an agreement and were now simply going over the details. "Casey, I never saw so many birds before. I can't keep track of them. I'm not really such a good flyer. I won't know what you lost or if I pull down any strays."

"Don't worry about it. I'll be here. You'll get used to it. It takes a little time, that's all. Don't worry about losing nothing, that's the name of the game. If you don't lose nothing for me

29

that means you ain't chasing 'em up. You gotta lose birds if you want to be good. You know that, right? You'll catch on. You just gotta work hard, though. There's a lot to do up here and I need someone I can count on. That's the main thing. Don't say you'll do it if you can't keep your word, okay?"

I nodded, to signify that I wouldn't say I'd do it until I was sure I could keep my word, but Casey misunderstood.

"Good," he said. He stood up, signaling an end to our conversation. "Meet me on the corner, ten o'clock Saturday. I'll make you a set of keys." And before I even had time to think about making a decision, I had become the chaser for one of the best flyers in all of Greenpoint and Williamsburg combined.

4

THE RUSSIAN CHURCH DOMINATED THE FAR END OF McCarren Park. It rose up across from the handball courts on North Twelfth Street, and its pale blond bricks were a sharp contrast to the dark tenements nearby. Its onion domes, capped with the milky green of weathered copper, made a distinct, exotic outline against the sky. When I looked at it from a distance, I could almost pretend I was in another world.

Its real name was the Cathedral of the Transfiguration of Our Lord, but everyone called it the Russian Church, and it had one outstanding eccentricity: its hourly bells were exactly ten minutes fast. They were so dependable that people set their clocks by them. On Saturday, I was already stationed in front of Reliable Fabricators when the bells chimed ten, so I knew I was early. I watched for the station wagon, although I had forgotten whether it was brown or dark green. I wondered if I would remember what Casey looked like, and

Jane Schwartz

smiled. I tried the outside door, but it was locked. I paced up
and down the block a dozen times, told myself that maybe I
hadn't pushed hard enough or turned the handle the right
way, and tried the door again. It was still locked.

After a while, a passing Buick slowed down. I started towards
it, thinking perhaps Casey had switched cars. When a clean-
shaven man leaned out to ask if anything was wrong, I ran
around the corner without answering.

I waited. I sat down on the sidewalk. I got up. I walked
around the block. I tried the door again. I began to wonder if I
had heard wrong. Maybe Casey had said twleve o'clock, or
even two. But I knew I was making excuses. I could hear his
very words: "Meet me on the corner, ten o'clock Saturday."

I refused to return home. It had been such a struggle getting
here. I had begged my mother for days. Frankie and Michael
also helped. They had been forced to return the pigeons to
Bennie, and after that they were soured on the sport. Frankie
said they had gotten too grown-up for it anyway. When I
commented on the suddenness of their growth, he refused to
respond. Still, he came up with a convincing argument in favor
of my chasing for Casey. He told Ma that he and Michael
were too busy for me anymore: they were in high school now,
they had football practice, they had started working out at
the Y. Ma taught English at P.S. 106 and then helped out
at the store so Junior could take on side jobs, mostly painting
and paneling—off the books—in the neighborhood. I would be
coming home to an empty apartment every afternoon. After
Mr. Corsini confirmed that he had heard of Casey, that he was
known in the neighborhood, Ma was almost persuaded. The
deciding factor, oddly enough, was Junior. He opposed the plan
too vehemently. As soon as he said I was absolutely forbidden

to go back on the roof, Ma got very quiet and left the room. For a moment, I almost felt sorry for Junior, because I knew then that he had lost. The next day Ma told me that a trial period was only fair. Provided that my schoolwork didn't suffer, I was entitled to have some fun.

Now, as the minutes stretched into an hour and the bells chimed a second time, I began to wonder if all these efforts had been in vain. Where was Casey? I couldn't stand on the corner all day. Finally, keeping a lookout for his car, I started walking. At first I had no clear sense where I was going, but when I got to Roebling an idea presented itself to me. I turned right and headed for the pigeon shop.

I almost lost my nerve several times along the way. What if they laughed at me? Or wouldn't let me in? After all, I had stolen someone's pigeons. Bennie might even be there. Maybe he was still mad. I walked more slowly. Even when I got there, I dawdled outside for a long time. I studied the show pigeons on display in the window. These were the fancy breeds that never flew: black-and-white Nuns with their neck feathers ruffled like a wimple; Trumpeters whose legs and feet were swirled with masses of feathers; Fantails who spread out their plumage like peacocks. Michael's father had a book with hundreds of pictures of them. They were pretty enough, I supposed, but too fussy for me. I preferred the Flights. And I didn't understand the point of a bird you couldn't fly.

Finally I went inside. "Hi," I said. I looked around. There was no one in the shop but Joey and a tall Puerto Rican boy, about Frankie's age, with his long skinny legs up on the card table. In the corner three kittens were lapping up milk from a broken dish.

33

"Hi. What can I do for you, dolly?" Joey mashed out his cigarette.

"Have you seen that guy Casey, by any chance?"

"Today, you mean?"

I nodded.

"Nah." Joey shook his head. "Hector, you seen Casey today?"

Hector shook his head. He was sprouting a wispy mustache that was so pale I hadn't noticed it a moment before. "I ain't seen him since we was playing cards down here on Wednesday. How come you want Casey?"

"He was supposed to meet me at his roof, to show me some things about the birds."

"You fly birds?" Hector lowered his feet to the floor.

I nodded.

"No kidding! I never knew no girl flying pigeons before. Joey, lemme have a cigarette, okay? I'll buy you some when I go out."

Joey reached across the counter and handed him a Camel. "What time was he supposed to meet you?" Joey asked.

"Around ten o'clock." I quickly added, "But I could have misunderstood or something."

Joey turned his back and started weighing out feed into small sacks. "Sometimes Casey forgets. Don't take it personal."

"Man, what you mean is, sometimes—by accident—Casey remembers." Hector laughed. "Don't worry." He slapped his bony hands against his knees. "He'll show up—*next* Saturday. Come on. You wanna go up on a roof? I'll take you up to my roof."

"I think I better stay here and wait, just in case."

"It's okay, dolly." Joey leaned over the counter. "If he comes in, I'll tell him you're at Hector's. He knows him. Go on.

You'll fly the birds. But Hector, you take her down when you're finished, okay? Walk her up to Metropolitan."

"Yeah, yeah. I know."

"But what am I supposed to do about Casey?" I asked. "He's expecting me."

Joey sighed. "Something probably came up. Don't worry. I know Casey for a long time. If you don't hear nothing, just go by his roof next Saturday." He nodded in Hector's direction. "Hector's a good boy. Go have fun. I'll remind Casey during the week."

I looked over at Hector. "You sure it's okay? You don't mind?"

"Nah. I'll show you my birds. I ain't got stock like Casey, but they fly."

"Okay." I turned back. "Thanks, Joey. By the way, my name's Louie." Joey bobbed his head and showed his missing tooth. I paused for a moment at the door, remembering that other night, the first time I had been there.

"Hey, Shorty, what're you waiting for?" Hector called out from the sidewalk.

Right in the center of my chest, I felt the bright warm glow of belonging.

5

THE FOLLOWING SATURDAY CASEY SHOWED UP AT THE
roof, just as Joey had predicted, although it was almost a quarter
to eleven when his station wagon pulled over to the curb. He
jumped out, jingling a set of keys at me. "Hey, what are you
drinking?"

"Nothing. Just some coffee." I crumpled up the empty paper
container. "I waited for you last week. Weren't you supposed
to meet me?"

Casey looked away. "Yeah, Joey told me. Something came up,
though. I couldn't get here. You understand that, right? You
ain't a baby. Come on, let me buy you another coffee." He
motioned for me to get up and I followed him across Bedford
into the luncheonette. "Hiya, babe," he said.

The girl behind the counter had a heavy face and her eyes
were thickly outlined in black. She looked up from her
newspaper and smiled. "Hi yourself, Casey." She peered over the

counter at me. This time she displayed more interest than
when I had gone in alone. "She's a little young even for you,
don't you think?"

"Don't get nasty, now." Casey grinned and pulled out his
wallet. "You like doughnuts?" He looked at me.

I nodded.

"Good. Let me have half a dozen of them doughnuts."

The girl lifted the plastic cover from the cake stand and
snapped open a brown paper sack. She pinched the doughnuts
two at a time, then half turned away and licked the flecks of
white glaze from her fingers.

"Anything else?"

"Yeah. Two coffees, one black and one—?"

"Half milk, with lots of sugar." I spoke directly to the girl,
but she looked at Casey.

He repeated my order. "How come you drink coffee anyway?
Aren't you too young for that stuff?"

"It's okay. It's the only way I drink milk."

"Is that a fact? Here, take this, willya?" He handed me the
bag. Glossy spots had already appeared where the doughnuts
pressed against the sides. He paid, and when the girl returned
his change, he gave her hand a quick squeeze.

We went out and walked over to the car. Casey set the
coffees down on the hood and opened the back door. Inside
was a wooden carrier, crowded with pigeons.

"I just picked these up over by the Engert Avenue shop. You
know the place? Near McGuinness?"

I shook my head. "The only shop I've ever been to is Joey's."

"You never been to the Engert store? You don't know Riley
and Kazoo and them guys?"

"Casey, I don't know anybody. I just started flying a few

37

months ago. I probably shouldn't even be here. I don't know hardly anything about the birds."

"Don't get so excited. Jesus Christ. I just asked you a question. I don't expect you to know everything. If you knew everything, you wouldn't need me in the first place. Just relax. Don't get all upset when I just ask you a question, okay?"

"Okay."

I didn't say anything as we climbed the stairs, but with each landing my doubts increased. Finally, on the top floor, before Casey could unlock the steel door, I whirled and faced him.

"Look, Casey, I'm really sorry but I don't think I belong here. I don't know enough about the birds, I don't even know who flies birds here in the neighborhood. I'm sorry if I acted like I did, maybe I shouldn't have said yes in the first place." I was short of breath, but I had to get it over with. Somehow, the truth hadn't sunk in. He didn't understand how ignorant I was or he never would have asked me to be his chaser in the first place.

Casey closed his eyes and muttered something to himself. "Look, why'd you say yes before?"

I thought for a minute. "Because I wanted to fly the birds. I wanted—I liked being up here."

"Okay, then. For the last time, I'm telling you, don't make such a production out of it. I'm here to teach you how to fly pigeons. You understand me? I'd just as soon you didn't know nothing. That way you'll learn the right way, not like these geeps around here. I had kids up here before, it wasn't worth the trouble training them. They think they're smart guys, they already know everything, they don't even listen to you. They don't show up, or they start trying to sneak the strays off the roof, sell them on their own. They're punks, you know what

I'm saying? They don't take no responsibility. I can't trust
them. But I got a feeling I can trust you, am I right?"

"Yeah. I guess so."

"All you gotta do is do what I tell you. Believe me, it'll get
easier every day, I promise. Just stop worrying all the time. I
never seen anybody worry as much as you. Remember, sweetheart, I asked you to come up here. I coulda had any kid on
the Northside chase for me. They'd all love to get their hands
on this stock, I got over four hundred birds up here, good
flying birds. But I picked you, understand? And you're not
gonna disappoint me, are you?"

I shook my head. I wanted very much not to disappoint him.

"I got a hunch about you," he went on. "You're good. You're
gonna do the right thing by me. We'll make a good team. Is it
a deal?" He extended his hand. I hesitated, then reached out.
His hand was warm and rough, and mine was swallowed up
inside it.

"Now do me a favor?"

I looked at him, ready to do anything he asked.

"Stop squashing them doughnuts. They're gonna be pancakes
when you get through with them." He tugged at the package
I had unconsciously been clutching against my chest.

"I'm sorry!"

"And stop saying you're sorry!"

"Okay, I'm sor—"

He hooted. "Come on. What are we talking out here for?
Let's get those birds out." This time I was prepared for the
flash of light as the door groaned open. I heard the mounting
gurgle of the birds and the ruffle of their wings. Even from
deep inside the coop, they could tell they had company.

Casey set down the coffees and pushed out another key with

his thumb. He stuck it in front of my nose. "This opens the outside door on the big coop, and this one"—he nudged a silver-colored key forward—"this here opens up the inside door where we keep the main stock. Go on. You open up."

I took the keys from him, carefully separating the two I needed from the rest of the bunch. The lock snapped open easily, but I had to twist the shackle at an extreme angle to wriggle it out of the link, because of a U-shaped metal housing structure that enclosed the lock on three sides.

Casey laughed at my contortions. "You know what that's for?"

"Unh-unh."

"In case anybody gets smart, tries to cut the lock. They been stealing them big metal clippers from the fire department, but they can't cut this lock 'cause they can't open up those clippers inside that shield I built."

The idea that anyone would go to such lengths to steal birds baffled me. For the first time, I realized that Frankie and Michael had been amateurs. Casey knew things they had never even thought of.

I ran my fingers over the bumpy seam that joined the shield to the steel coop. "How did you do that?"

"What do you mean? I welded it on."

"How did you know how to do that?"

"That's my job, babe. I'm a welder. That's what I do for a living. I built this whole coop outta steel."

"Oh."

"I used to work for the T.A. as a matter of fact, over at the main yard. Sometimes I think I shoulda stood there, you know, for the pension and everything. But I got tired of it. Anyway, I work over at another place now, a small shop over near Bushwick. We get sent out on a lotta jobs, you don't have to stay in the shop all the time. I like that better than staying in one place every day." He pushed me around to face the door again. "Come on, babe. You're taking all day to get this lock off. The birds is gonna starve by the time you get in there to feed them."

The second lock, once I was inside, was much easier to open. The birds were in full chorus by now. Urgent, throbbing sounds welled up from behind the door. I looked over at Casey and he nodded.

I was to see it hundreds of times, but I never got used to it. The entire stock cascading through a narrow doorway, their wings snapping like sheets in the wind as they swirled into the screen and surrounded me.

Casey chuckled. "Don't get scared now. They ain't gonna hurt you. Here." He waded into the middle of the throng of birds that now occupied the entire floor. "Let's get them all the way outside for some real exercise." He shooed the pigeons out, leaning over towards the ones scattered on the ground and waving his arms to clear out the rest that were skittering around overhead.

"I can't believe how many birds there are!" We stood side by side as the entire stock congregated on the top of the coop, bobbing and weaving among one another as they pecked the empty tarpaper in search of food.

"They're hungry, the little geeps. Look at them. There ain't no food out there, you dummies! You gotta move first! You gotta get a little exercise."

Bending over, he pulled up the long bamboo chasing pole and swept the birds right off the coop, tapping the pole against the corner to shake up the slowpokes who were reluctant to flap off.

41

He whistled sharply and they spiraled out against the sky. Without shifting his gaze, he began pointing things out.

"Most of these geeps around here don't hardly fly their birds no more. Look around. Like now, there ain't no other stocks up but ours. We send our birds up regardless, understand? If there's a million stocks out, send the pigeons up. If the wind's blowing directly over Bennie's or Tito's or Angelo's, I don't care. Send 'em up. Be a sport. Get a little action going. I don't ever want to hear that you're a mutt, like the rest of these bastards, okay? Don't be afraid. I don't care what you lose. If you get a little action, if you have fun up here, that's what it's all about, okay?"

I nodded.

"And another thing. Even if there's nobody out, you send the birds up and make them work. Unless it's raining hard or snowing, they go up. No excuses. Now, in the mornings, just a quick fly, and for a while, if it stays nice, you can leave them out bumming all day till you get done with school. But if it's ugly out, or real cold, then go ahead and lock them up during the day. After school, you can really chase them. That's when most of the action is anyway during the week. In the afternoon. I'll be coming up around four, four-thirty, when I get outta work. I'll teach you how to use the net and everything. You ever use a hoople? You catch any strays over there?"

"Not really. We flew off a fire escape, and Michael said they'd never come down on a place like that, even if we could've hooked them up."

"That's probably true. Anyway, you'll get plenty up here. If you can't handle the net, just let 'em hang around and walk 'em in later on with the pole. Pull the trap open and walk 'em in. That's okay. You'll lose plenty, too. That's to be expected. Just try to notice what goes lost, if you can, and if you can ever spot where they go down. I got a pair of binoculars over by the feed bin, take a look around. After a while you'll be able to see pretty much without them."

"But, Casey, how am I supposed to recognize them? You've got a million pigeons up here. It's not like before. We had thirty-four birds! That was different. I knew every one of them."

"I thought I told you not to worry so much."

"But, Case, I'm serious. I'll get all mixed up."

"Jesus Christ, will you just relax! I never saw anyone worry so much in my entire life. I told you already, I'm gonna show you. You'll get used to everything if you don't take a heart attack the first time you come up! I'm telling you, you spend every day up here with me, you'll learn things guys down at the store flying pigeons forty years don't even know. Just trust me, willya? Just keep your eyes and ears open. The pigeons is gonna teach you themselves. You'll see. Okay, babe?"

I nodded.

"Now. You got any questions?"

"Yeah. How do I know how much to feed them?"

"Look here." He led me over to the shanty and opened the metal trunk that held the feed sacks. "Take this coffee can for a dipper and give them about three or four cans in the morning after they fly. I'll feed them in the afternoon. And make sure the water pail is full. Pigeons like to drink. They like water. I'll show you how to do that 'cause it's different, you use a special pail."

"Don't you just use that trough there?"

"Not really. That there is for bathing so they can clean themselves. That stays outside the coop."

"But they drink out of it! I saw them!"

Casey laughed. "Sure they drink out of it. What are you gonna do, put a sign up and tell 'em, ' 'Scuse me, pigeons, that's only for bathing?' "

I bit my tongue.

"Anyway," he went on, "they got special pails for inside that don't spill. I'll show you. No big deal. What else do you want to know?"

I rummaged through the odds and ends jammed into the feed trunk. "What's this?" I held up a sack of peach-colored crystals, but Casey was no longer listening to me. He was staring off into the sky, half in and half out of the shanty. Suddenly, he snatched up the bamboo pole and raced over to the coop. "Gyyaaaaaaaahh!!" he shouted. "Go on, get up there! Move!" The whole stock ripped off the roof, dove out of sight for a second and then reappeared, the tumult of their wings growing fainter as they rolled out into the distance. I ran over next to him.

"There's a stray up there. You see it?"

I squinted in the direction he pointed but saw only his own stock.

"It's a Dutch silver beard, he's coming back. Watch over there when he turns."

I caught a quick flash, like the glint from a ring. "That's not a bird, is it, Casey?"

"That's it, babe. Now we gotta try and get these turkeys over there and hook it up. Can you whistle?"

"Not really."

Casey put his fingers in his mouth and practically blasted me off the roof. "If you can't whistle, then yell at 'em, okay? You gotta make noise, make 'em move. Yaa-ooooooopppp!! Yaaahhoop!"

I couldn't help giggling.

"Whatsa matter?" Casey chuckled. "This is the Wild West up here, baby. You gotta get used to it. Don't be shy now. Yell at those pigeons! Get them going!"

I cleared my throat. When Casey whistled the next time I yelled "Gyyaaa! Go on!" My feeble cries embarrassed me, and I resolved to practice when I was alone. The wind was blowing away from the roof, so the stock naturally drifted with it towards the east. As they approached the stray, Casey flicked me on the shoulder with the back of his hand. "Watch 'em now. Maybe they'll hook him up."

"Do they know what they're doing, Case?"

"What do you mean?"

"I mean, are they going after him on purpose?"

"Naw, they don't really go after each other. We're the competitors, not them. They just go with the wind or they get into some pattern. They'll stick together though, that's the thing. They got an instinct—the flock-pull, or some people call it the kit-pull—that tells them to stick with the other birds for protection. They're born with it, then you reinforce it through the training. Like in the fall, especially, when you start breaking in the young birds, you watch when you send them up, and if there's a bird that goes off on his own or something, you have to cull him, twist his neck, or give him away or whatever."

"How do you get them to catch the stray?"

"You just do your best. There's only so much a flyer can do. The kit-pull works on the stray, too. He's got that same instinct to hook up with the flock for protection, and at the same time, he's got a homing instinct that tells him to get back to his own roof. The two instincts are kinda like at war. The stock'll go wherever they feel like it, all you can do is wave

45

the flag or holler or clap to try to startle them off in a certain direction. Otherwise they'll just go with the wind, or if there's something else in the sky—gulls or a plane or something—they get spooked real easy into a different direction. Sometimes, if there's a lot of stocks out and you really want to scramble them up, you might even toss up a couple of cherry bombs."

"Cherry bombs?"

"Yeah. You ain't never heard of them?"

"They're firecrackers, right?"

"Yeah. But don't worry though." He fixed me with his eyes, reading my mind. "I do all the firecrackers up here. You don't have to touch nothing. I don't want nobody else up here setting anything off, okay? Now. Any more questions?"

"Yeah. What do you do with the birds you catch? Do you give them back or what?"

"Are you crazy? This here is strictly catch-keep. That's the only way I play. Whatever we catch up here, that's ours, free and clear. Don't listen to none of them crybabies down at the shop asking for this one back or the other one. They're all schmockers anyway. You can't trust 'em. They agree to play free-catch, or catches where you buy your birds back, then they lie like crazy and say they didn't catch nothing on you. Don't ever let me hear you went crying for something you lost, okay? Whatever you lose here is gone forever. That's it. Say 'Good-bye, pigeon, have a nice life.' That's the only way I play the game. A lotta these geeps spend the whole day driving around, getting their birds back. It don't make sense. So what if you pay a dollar to get them back? There's no risk there. You ever play poker?"

I shook my head.

"Well, it's like playing poker and then when the game's over, everybody gets their money back. There's no point to it. It's gotta be for keeps, Louie. That's what makes it a sport, that's where the excitement comes in. If you're the type of person that gets upset because someone catches one of your birds, you shouldn't be up here. 'Cause that's a way of life here, you know what I mean? The guy that taught me, he was a real old-timer. He told me this saying: 'You catch, you lose. You lose, you catch.' Either way, that's the end of it. You understand?"

"Okay."

"And I'll tell you another thing. I don't even *want* them back if they get caught. You know why? Because they're not reliable. If they went lost once, chances are they'll do it again. We tested them one year, me and Fingers, when he was still coming up with me, 'cause I'll be honest with you, I don't have the kind of patience he does to check out something like that. But we took back forty-two pigeons that had gone down on the various roofs and mixed them back in, and forty-one of them went down again within a week, I swear to god. Forty-one went right back down. So you're not even doing yourself a favor. That's all there is to it. It's the only way it makes sense. Catch-keep." He paused. "I'm talking too much, you know that? I talked to you more already than I talked home in a whole week."

Before I could answer, something distracted him. I saw him shift his gaze to the doorway, and turned to see a heavyset man standing on the roof, looking casually up at the birds. His dark hair was slicked back and he wore a leather jacket the color of caramel. His trousers had sharp creases, his black shoes shone. I could tell by his clothes that he had not come on the roof to fly pigeons.

"Hey, babe!" Casey called out and the stranger nodded.

"Louie, listen. You go on home now. That's enough for today."

"But, Case, it's still early!"

"Listen to me." He squeezed my shoulder. "You come up Monday after school, okay? We'll take it from there." Before I realized it, he had guided me over to the door. "And you remember what I said, okay?" He gave me a push towards the stairs.

"About what? Catch-keep?"

But Casey didn't answer. His focus was on the stranger. I had been dismissed.

6

ALTHOUGH JUNIOR AND MY MOTHER WERE THE SAME
age—he had turned thirty-six in September, exactly one week
after Ma—I thought of him as a much older man. His wiry
black hair was already streaked with grey, and he had deep
circles under his eyes. Soon after he shaved, a dark stubble
appeared along his jaw, so that his face seemed always heavy
and worn. His size added to this impression. Only a few
inches over five feet, he had a great barrel chest and massive
arms. He wasn't fat, but his body weighted him down; inside
the house he moved awkwardly and with care, aware of some
disadvantage to his bulk.

My mother was the opposite, light and quick. She had
Frankie's coloring, and her hair hung loose and wavy around
her face. Except for lipstick, she wore very little makeup. Her
only vanity was her hands. They were beautifully tended, each
nail a perfect oval and always painted bright red.

I don't know when she had time to care for her nails. Both she and Junior worked constantly that year. They were home only on those rare nights when Junior's sister-in-law volunteered to relieve them at the store.

I had been given a six o'clock curfew, but because my comings and goings went largely unnoticed, I had been extending it little by little. My luck held for about three weeks, and then one night it ran out. I walked into the apartment to find Ma, Frankie, and Junior sitting around the table, eating dinner together.

"Oh—hi." I hung my key on its nail.

"Where the devil have you been, Louise? Do you know what time it is?"

I squinted at the clock over the stove. "It's a quarter to seven." I avoided Junior's eyes and slipped into my chair without taking off my jacket.

"Don't get smart, young lady. You know what Junior means."

"Ma, it's not even seven o'clock. What's the big deal?"

"Seven o'clock's not the point," Junior broke in. "And this isn't the first time either, I'm sure of that. You're spending too much time over on that roof. Ever since you started up there you're never home no more."

"Well, no one else is either. I'm busy. I'm helping out at Joey's too, you know. He pays me. It's a job."

"Well, it's getting dark now, and I don't like you coming in this late. You know, people get worried about you when you don't show up, or didn't you ever think about that?"

I sighed and stared into my empty plate. The reflection of the overhead light appeared in the center of it, forming a sharp yellow disk the size of a quarter with a hazy ring around it. I leaned forward to look at my face, but then my head blocked the bulb and all I could see was my silhouette.

"Louise, did you hear Junior?"

I kept my eyes on the plate. "I'm sorry, *Ma*. I had to bag feed at Joey's. It took longer than I thought."

"Louie, you can't spend your whole life on that goddamn roof!"

I looked at Ma. She didn't allow cursing in the house, but this time she didn't correct Junior. "Why can't I?" I said.

"For one thing, you're supposed to be home. If you'd be home, you could at least help your mother get dinner on the table."

"Well, if she didn't have to work at your store all the time there wouldn't be any problem."

"Damn it, Louie, do you have any idea why your mother's working so hard in the first place?"

"Junior!" Ma's voice carried a warning. "Louie, you listen to me and you listen good. I don't *have* to work anywhere I don't want. You understand that? Nobody's making me."

"Anyway," I said, "why can't Frankie help?"

"Frankie does other things."

"Yeah? Like what?"

Frankie put down his fork. "I take out the trash."

"Big deal."

"It is, too. It's more work than you do."

"Yeah?"

"Yeah."

"Good, then let's trade. I'll take out the trash and you help Ma."

Junior motioned for Frankie to keep quiet. "Louie, I don't want you taking out the trash. Why can't you do just one

51

thing that girls are supposed to do, would you mind telling me that? Just once. Most girls like to help out in the kitchen and go shopping and get dressed up. Why can't you do stuff like that after school instead of chasing pigeons? It ain't right. Why don't you go out with your girlfriends for a change?"

I thought for a moment. "I don't have any girlfriends. Pass the bread. *Please*."

Junior handed me the loaf of Italian bread and a plate of butter. "Why not?"

"I don't like girls."

"Louie!" Ma's eyes widened. "That's not true!"

"Yes, it is. Except Paulette, maybe. I liked Paulette okay."

Paulette had been my best friend in second and third grade, but her family had moved back to North Carolina two years ago. I'd only seen her once since then, when she'd come to visit her aunt during the summer. We didn't even write, except at Christmas.

"Aw, that's terrific." Junior tipped his chair back from the table. "Couldn't you at least pick one that wasn't a nigger?"

"Ma, did you hear what he said!"

"Do not use that word in my house!"

"Your house?" Junior reddened but did not back down. "Excuse me. I'm only telling the truth. What's the matter with that? The fact is, the only people your daughter hangs out with are niggers and bums. Now if that don't bother you, fine. That's fine with me."

"They are not bums!" I shouted.

"Who says? The only ones that ain't bums are gangsters. I grew up with these guys and I know more about them than you ever will."

"Oh, yeah? What do you know? I'll bet you never even went up on one of their roofs!"

"I'm not talking about roofs! I'm talking about the real world, that's what I'm worried about. You don't know these guys like I do. You don't know what's going on there in these so-called pet shops."

"There's nothing going on there! There's pigeons, that's what's going on. Don't believe him, Ma! I'm at Joey's almost every day. There's nothing wrong there. Tell him!"

"That's enough from both of you! Now just stop it!"

Junior's tone changed. "Honey, I'm just thinking about Louie. She's growing up, if you know what I mean, and I think she should be more careful who she spends her time with, that's all."

"I'll spend my time with whoever I want. You can't tell me what to do."

"Louise, don't you dare speak like that to Junior!"

"But, Ma, I'm not doing anything bad. I swear! I promise I'm not doing anything wrong."

"I'm not talking about you." Junior turned back to my mother. "I'm talking about these two-bit hoods that hang around the pet shops. I know these guys. They're in with Mickey Leg over on Meeker Avenue and guys like Ray Tertullo. I told you you shouldn't let her start with them in the first place."

"I didn't let her 'start' with anybody! Now that's enough. I do not want to discuss this at the dinner table, if you don't mind."

"I'm just telling you what's going on. You don't seem to understand these guys she's hanging out with."

53

"But I'm not hanging out, Ma! I'm just learning how to fly the birds."

"It's the same thing," Junior said.

"It is *not* the same thing! It's the complete opposite! It's a sport, that's all. It's not a crime. You don't even understand the first thing about flying birds!"

"And you don't understand the first thing about anything!"

"That's enough, both of you!" My mother slammed her chair back. Junior and I shut up. "Junior, we'll talk about this later, in private. Louie, eat your dinner."

I tore off a piece of bread and buttered it, then pushed it around absentmindedly before pulling it apart into three uneven sections. Frankie was watching me, but no one said anything. The silence expanded, like air filling a balloon, until I thought the room would explode. I started chewing on the bread.

"Ugh! Ma, that's disgusting! Look at her. Can't you make her wash her hands or something?"

Ma looked over at my plate. The bread was marbled with oily grey streaks. "Louie, go wash your hands, please, sweetheart. And why don't you take off your jacket while you're up and make yourself at home, okay?"

I stared at the bread for a minute, then walked over to the sink.

The rest of the meal was ruined. I loved Ma's spaghetti and meatballs, but I had no appetite left. Junior tried to make up to me by urging me to eat; otherwise no one said a thing. Finally, to make him stop talking, I took one meatball and spooned sauce over it. I mashed it up and spread it out all over my plate, but I never got around to putting any of it into my mouth.

After a while, Frankie cleared his throat. "What's for dessert?"

Ma went over to the pantry and opened a bag of Oreos. I watched Junior and Frankie eat. When we were little, Frankie always used to separate his Oreos and lick the icing off the one half first, then eat the chocolate wafers, until one day Michael told him that was the sissy way to eat them. Now Frankie ate them like everyone else.

"Want some coffee, honey?" For just a second, Ma rested her hand on the back of Junior's neck.

"Please," he said. "Thanks." He pushed his plate away and leaned forward. "Come on, Louie, don't be mad. I love you kids. Someday you'll understand. I'm just trying to look after my family." He smiled at me. Bits of black cookie were stuck between his teeth.

"You're not my family." My voice was so low that for a second no one, including myself, seemed quite sure I had said it.

"Louie!" Ma took a step forward and stopped.

"Well, he's not! Not really." I glanced back and forth at both of them. The color had drained from Junior's face. "I'm only telling the truth." I mimicked his earlier outburst. "What's the matter with that? Don't you want me to tell the truth anymore?"

"Louise, that's enough!"

"Well, it's true!" I cried. "He's not my family and he never will be my family and anyway I hate him anyway!" I kicked back my chair and ran down the hall.

I yanked the curtain across my room and rifled through my drawers until I found the masking tape. I ripped off a long strip and taped the curtain to the wall on one side. I tore off another piece and fastened the other side. I kept on ripping, piece after piece, until the roll was empty and my hands were covered with curls of tape. Then I rubbed them off onto the linoleum.

My stomach started to rumble. I hadn't eaten for hours, but nothing in the world could have made me go back into that kitchen. I crawled under the covers and pulled my knees tight against my chest. I could feel my insides knotting up around the emptiness. I had been hungry before, but I had never been so hungry that it hurt, and I began to wonder how hungry you had to be before you died.

7

HECTOR KEPT HIS BIRDS ON THE ROOF OF AN
abandoned building overlooking the Williamsburg Bridge. His coop
was a ramshackle affair, pieced together from wood scraps and
chicken wire. Even I could have demolished it with a few
well-placed kicks.

He had a small stock, maybe twenty Flights, and four Racing
Homers that weren't very good. It wasn't Hector's fault. He
didn't have a car, so he couldn't train them properly. He had to
take them by carrier in the subway; as a result, the most
they'd ever flown was from Coney Island or the Bronx back to
Williamsburg. That wasn't very far, considering that even the
local races were fifty to a hundred miles. But Hector spent a lot
of time on those birds, and that year he had entered his best
cock in the Turkey Race, which took place the day before
Thanksgiving. Twenty-three other flyers had also entered, at a
dollar apiece. Joey took me with him to Waldbaum's to select

the prizes: a twenty-pound. Butterball for the winner, and two smaller birds for second and third place.

Fingers was the only flyer everybody trusted, so he was elected to drive the pigeons out to Montauk in his van. For official competitions they had to hire a bonded truck driver, but the Turkey Race was just for fun, something Joey had organized years ago, when he first took over the pet shop.

Normally, I didn't care about such races. They were for the Homer guys, and our roof was strictly Flights. But I was pulling for Hector because he was my friend, and as soon as school was out on Wednesday I dashed over to the pet shop to wait for the results.

The sun had been playing hide-and-seek for days, but that afternoon was pure gold, with a sharp chill in the air. It was perfect flying weather. The first bird made it home in record time. It belonged to a man named Tommy Parelli, and it reached his roof a little before three-thirty. Tito was second, and Butchie the Old Man came in third. They were all regulars at Joey's shop. Two more of Tommy's birds made it back in the first ten, and when he showed up at the shop he brought along a bottle of whiskey. He gave me fifty cents to buy soda and candy so I could celebrate with the rest of them.

When Hector still hadn't shown up by five-thirty, I began to get worried. Everyone said he could just forget about his bird—it wasn't coming back after dark. They said Hector had probably gone home for dinner long ago. But I knew Hector better than that. He was stubborn. He'd stay up on that roof all night if he had to.

I congratulated Tommy once more and grabbed my coat. I was halfway out the door when Joey stopped me. "If you're going by Hector's, be careful," he said. "Stick your head in on the way home."

I ran all the way. The worst part was the corner of South Fourth, where the Spanish Knights hung out. I flew past them, and when I reached Hector's building, on the next block, I was gasping for breath. There were no lights inside. I picked my way over the rubble in the hallway and stumbled up the four flights.

"Hector!" I hollered as I neared the top.

That one word saved my life. I stepped onto the roof and looked straight into the barrel of a gun.

"Damn you, Shorty! What the hell are you doing sneaking up like that?" Hector was shaking all over as he lowered his arm.

I couldn't believe my eyes. "Is that *real*?"

"Yeah, it's real! You coulda got killed, damn you!"

I stared at the silver-and-white pistol in his hand. It was so small, it looked like a toy. "Let me see, Hector."

Hector backed off. "Don't play around, Shorty. It's a .22, and it's loaded."

"But Hector, what are you doing with a gun? Are you okay?"

"I always got a gun up here. I been robbed too many times."

"I didn't know that."

"There's a lot of things you don't know."

"Did they take your birds?"

"Once. They take nickels and dimes around here. Anything. I'm sick of all of them."

"I got worried. You didn't come down. We figured your bird went lost by now."

"He ain't lost, Shorty. Something happened. I know that bird. He's coming home."

"But Hector, how late can you stay up here? Tommy said the birds hardly ever come in after dark."

"He'll come in. I know it. I'm waiting till that bird gets home. It ain't the race. I know I lost behind everybody. I don't care. It's just that bird. I gotta wait for him."

"Are you okay though?"

"I'm all right. You go home, Shorty. I don't want you up here when he comes back. You might spook him, you know. They can tell if someone strange is here, or anything's different. He might not land. I'll see you tomorrow." He got the flashlight from inside the coop and followed me to the stairs. "I'll hold this while you go down. Don't worry. I'll watch you from the roof, it's okay. But don't ever come up like that again, Shorty. Yell up from the street first, okay? Don't surprise me no more."

"Good night, Hector," I said. "I'm sorry. I hope your bird comes home."

I raced back up Roebling, waved at Joey through the window, and raced home. Luckily, no one was there.

The next morning was even more beautiful. I fed the birds and left them bumming outside. When I got to the pet shop it was still early, but already there was a crowd.

"Look over here." Joey made a space for me and I squeezed in. Hector was leaning over a box in the center of the table. Inside it was his bird. Hector was beaming. "I told you, Shorty," he smiled. "He's alive."

"What happened, Hector? Tell me."

"He got his chest tore open by a chicken hawk or something. He flew back like that, cut open. About eighty-thirty I heard something, he just fell down on the coop. He was bleeding and everything, but he made it. It's like a miracle."

"Is he gonna live?"

"I think so," Hector said. "I brought him over here right away and Joey gave him the antibiotic. Fingers called this friend of his, this pharmacist. He's got birds, and he came over right away and sewed up his chest. He thinks he's gonna be okay."

"Oh, Hector." I touched his arm. I had never seen him look so happy.

Butchie started telling us stories about all the Homers he'd known that had straggled in through hailstorms, or with broken wings, or bleeding feet. Butchie exaggerated sometimes, and I never knew whether to believe him or not. But I believed this: Hector's bird had flown back from Montauk with his chest ripped open. I was seeing it with my own two eyes.

I repeated the story to Casey as soon as he got up on the roof. He laughed. He knew all about Hector's "miracle." He'd been at Joey's the night before and seen everything. He bet me a million dollars that every Thanksgiving for the next twenty years, they'd be telling the story of Hector's Homer for some new flyer, and before long Hector's name would be known all over the neighborhood.

Casey was in a great mood that morning. He spread his arms out and whirled around. "This is a perfect day, ain't it sweetheart? Am I telling the truth or what? It's perfect flying weather. Even the birds is thankful today." He was right. Our birds floated through the sky in perfect unison, tight as a fist. They rolled out and back time and time again and didn't seem the least bit tired. By one o'clock we had caught fourteen strays.

I got home in plenty of time to help out with Thanksgiving. I set the table while Frankie made a fruit punch with ginger ale. Ma had stuffed the turkey with sausage dressing, and we had twice-baked potatoes with melted cheese, and peas and onions, and pumpkin pie. Junior and I even got along. For one whole day, everyone I knew was happy.

8

I WAS STARING AT THE BIRDS SO INTENTLY AS THEY
streamed up Bedford Avenue that I didn't even hear Casey till
he was right behind me.

"What do you got here?" He took the pole from me and
walked towards the coop, scanning the sky.

I followed and pointed just beyond where he was looking.
"There's two of Gus's, I think. A blue checker and an Isabella
cap. And a silver dun—I don't know *who* she belongs to."

"Oh, yeah?" Casey kept his eyes on the birds. "You're getting
to know everybody pretty good, huh?"

I nodded. I didn't really *know* most of the flyers, not
personally. I just knew their names and where their roofs
were. That was all that mattered.

"You catch anything yet?" Casey said.

"Just a strawberry." I tried to sound casual. "Look." I tugged
at his sleeve and pointed to the holding pen. "See?"

He glanced over quickly and nodded. "Very nice," he drawled, "very nice." He swept away a half-dozen birds that were already circling back towards the roof. "What's the matter with these turkeys? They can't be tired already." He looked sideways at me. "You just got up here, right?"

"Go on, *git*!" I ran over to the coop and pounded on the roof with my fists. "Git up there, you birds! Go on, fly!" They flapped reluctantly off.

"Man, these pigeons look *dead*. You sure you just got up here?"

"Yeah. Where'd you work today, Case? You still over on India Street?"

Casey ignored me. He tossed the pole aside and shaded his eyes. "Yep. They sure look dead to me. You know, we was driving by about one o'clock, I hadda pick up something on Bayard, and I coulda swore I saw our birds chargin' up, and that same little silver dun was flying right over them. She's one tough little hen, ain't she?"

"She's incredible!" I turned towards him in a rush, then stopped myself.

"Uh-huh!" Casey grunted. "And you been up here all day tryin' to catch her, right?"

I didn't answer.

"You didn't go to school or nothing, am I right?"

"Casey, I swear I'll never do it again!" I grabbed his arm with both hands. "I promise, honest I won't! I didn't even mean to. I was just gonna feed 'em and lock 'em up this morning when she went by, and I said I'm just gonna send 'em up this *once*, and see if they could bring her down. And then they almost did but she broke away. So I was gonna go in, but then she flew by a second time, and I knew I'd get

63

her-then, so I sent 'em up one more time, and they stayed up a long time and hooked her up and everything, but then they lost her again. So then I was really sure I'd get her the next time, but she disappeared for a while and I had to wait, and by then it was so late anyhow ..."

Casey was shaking his head slowly back and forth. I pushed him around to face west.

"She came back that way, from the city, I don't know, but I think she's got double blue bands like Mooney's. You think she's one of Mooney's, Case?" I didn't wait for an answer. "See, if I just had another chance, I know I could get her. I hooked her up three or four times already. One time she even dropped. She landed and everything!"

"Hey. *Hey*." Casey pried my fingers loose from his left arm. He grinned down at me. "Yeah, go on," he teased. "She landed and then what? How come you didn't catch her?"

"I tried, Case, I swear, but she took off again right away. I didn't even get over there and she was gone."

"You try to walk her in or what?"

"No, Case, come on. I had the hoople and everything, but she just took off. I didn't even take two steps."

"You gotta learn to handle that net, babe." He spoke slowly, spacing his words far apart. "You're gonna keep on losing birds like this." He squeezed the upper part of my right arm. "You're too scrawny. You don't got no muscle there."

I shook him off and backed away a few steps.

"That net's too heavy for you, ain't it?"

"It is *not*! Nobody could've caught her. I told you, she took off right away. That's why I had to stay up all day, I was trying to make her drop again."

"Oh, yeah, I forgot. You *had* to stay up with the pigeons all day, right? You just *had* to skip school and stay up on the roof since seven o'clock this morning. That's good. That's really good." He leaned over the side of the roof and spit. "You didn't go down all day or what?"

I shook my head.

"You eat anything?"

"I had my lunch."

"That's some life ya got. A good life for a *bum*." He was quiet for a minute, chewing on his forefinger. Then he jerked it from his mouth and pointed it at me. "Don't you *ever* let me catch you skippin' school to come up on the roof, understand?"

I nodded.

"You wanna be a bum or what?"

"No, Case, honest. It just happened."

"I got enough troubles already, lettin' you come up here. I don't need no more."

"Casey, I swear. I only did it for that one bird. I promise I won't do it again. I *swear*!"

"Okay, okay. Calm down. I just don't want no trouble. You belong in school, okay?"

"Okay. But Case?"

"What's the matter?"

"You used to skip school *all* the time. You told me yourself."

"That's different. That was a long time ago. Things was— everything was different."

The pigeons had landed again, and Casey shifted his attention to the coop.

"You see the blue checker?"

I stood on my toes to get a better look. "In the back there?"

"That's right," Casey crooned. "Hand me the net, willya, sweetheart?"

65

I reached down and grabbed the net, slipping it to Casey without a sound. He covered the roof in long, silent strides. A few feet from the coop he switched the hoople to his left hand, keeping it close to his body. He walked over to the far end of the coop, his eyes riveted on the blue checker stray. For an instant, he was absolutely still, like a cat gauging the distance to its prey. Then he gripped the edge of the coop with one large hand, gave a quick jump, and swung his left arm in a perfect arc. The hoople landed squarely over the blue before it even knew what hit him. Casey grabbed the bird from under the net and stretched his hand back without looking around. I was there, waiting. I took the stray over to the back coop and tossed him in the holding pen.

"You see that?" he called out from across the roof, waving the net. "That's how you catch *birds*, woman!" He ran over to me and made a wild attempt to trap me in the net. "Like this!"

I screamed and tried to back away, but he cornered me against the wall. "You just spot a little stray in there where she don't belong and *whoosh!*" He brought the net down over my head.

"No, nooo!" I laughed and crouched down, trying to wriggle out.

"Okay, okay." He tossed the net aside and ruffled my hair. "You look just like some of them strays." He laughed. "Like Mooney's birds!"

"I do not!" I bristled at the insult.

"Yeah, you do. Just like 'em. They don't got no meat on 'em and neither do you." He reached out and pinched my waist.

"Owww!" I slapped at him and he laughed again.

"Only he don't *feed* his birds, that's why they're so damn thin, and you—you eat like a lumberjack! I seen you *inhale* doughnuts up here, I swear to god. I don't know how your old man affords to feed you even with the grocery store!" He grabbed for me again, but I stiffened and turned away.

"He's not my old man."

Casey stopped smiling. "Aw, don't be so damn touchy."

"Well, he's *not*."

Casey didn't answer.

"Anyway, you're the one getting fat around here!" I turned back and snatched at Casey's belly, but he caught my wrist and twisted it behind my back. "Ow! *Ow!* Casey, let go, that hurts!"

He grinned and relaxed his hold. "Then take that back," he ordered. "Go on, take it back."

"Un-unh," I laughed, trying to pull away. "*Ow!* Okay, okay, I take it back." He let go and I rubbed my wrist. "I just meant that your wife feeds you okay, Case, that's all."

"Yeah." Casey glanced at his watch. His voice had gone flat.

"What's the matter?"

"Nothin'."

"Case?"

He stuck the hoople on a nail and scooped up a canful of corn. "Come on," he said, avoiding my bewildered look. "Let's feed 'em and lock 'em up."

"But, Case, what about the silver dun? She's still up there."

Casey hesitated.

"Can't we try just once more, Case? I'm sure *you* could get her. *Please*."

Casey glanced at his watch again, then back up at the sky. A mile away, like a cinder caught in a draft, the dun was drifting towards New York. I moved a step closer, and we both squinted against the late afternoon sun.

"I'm supposed to be someplace." Casey didn't take his eyes off the bird. I kept my mouth shut. "I'm supposed to take my old lady shopping."

Still, he kept watching the sky. Suddenly, he reached down for the pole and ran over to the coop, cutting out almost thirty birds and chasing them up. He clapped and whistled sharply. "Git up now!" he hollered after them. "Git up there!"

"Where is she, Case? I lost her."

He turned me roughly by the shoulder so I was facing farther south. I strained my eyes. It was already dusk, and everything was getting harder to distinguish. I tried to focus, knowing the bird would appear again when the light struck it just right.

"*Way* up," Casey said, squeezing my shoulders. "See her now?"

A few seconds passed. "Yes!" I cried. "Look how high she is!"

Casey put his fingers in his mouth and split the air with another whistle. The rest of the birds took off and swooped low over the edge two or three times before they dared to return. The group he'd sent up were climbing, but very slowly.

He rested his hand on my shoulder again. I didn't move. "I don't know," he mused. "I just don't know. These turkeys look awful wore out to me."

It was a reprimand and I knew it. Not for tiring the birds—nobody worked them harder than Casey—but for skipping school to stay up on the roof all day. But I could tell he wasn't really mad anymore.

"They'll get her, Case, I know they will. They'll hook her up again. She's got to get tired too."

"Well, we'll see." It was out of our hands now. We walked over to the top step and sat down. All we could do was watch.

"You really like them little silver duns, huh, babe?" He looked over at me, then back up at the sky. I nodded, and we both leaned back in silence, gazing at the birds.

After a while, I asked, "Did you ever have a favorite, Case?"

"What do you mean? A favorite *color* bird or a favorite bird?"

"I don't know. A favorite color?"

Casey leaned forward, resting his elbows on his knees, and thought for a minute. "Yeah. Isabellas, I guess. They were— how would you say that? They were more—*unusual* then. A lot of people didn't keep 'em in those days. Not so much like now. Now everybody's got Isabellas, even that geep across the way raises them. He sold a hundred of them last summer to Tito's brother-in-law out on the Island. But what the hell, that's all he does now anyway, right? He's a fucking breeder, that's all, 'cause he sure as hell don't *fly* his birds no more."

"But what about a favorite bird, Case? Did you ever have like just a favorite *bird*?"

"Oh, yeah. Sure." He stood up. "Everybody does when they're kids. Who remembers what it was? That was five hundred years ago. That was another lifetime."

He walked off to the back of the roof. I started to follow him, then thought better of it. I wandered over to the holding pen and studied the two strays for a while. The strawberry had calmed down long ago and was busy picking mites out from the base of his feathers. He'd grasp the shaft in his beak and then take three or four quick little nips along the ridge, pause, then start with the next stem. The blue was still scared. He perched on the near ledge with one eye staring out the wire, his chest pounding. I wondered if his heart was larger or smaller than the tip of my thumb. From the corner of my eye, I noticed Casey untangling the hose out behind the elevator shaft. I knew the stock was heading back, but I told myself that if I didn't look, they'd stay up just a little longer and hook up the dun.

After a minute, Casey called out, "They're coming down, babe. Go feed 'em and let's get outta here."

But even after the birds were all locked up, I kept looking for the dun. Casey finally put his jacket on and was jingling his keys.

"Let's go, kiddo. She ain't comin' down."

"But where's she gonna go?"

"How the hell am I supposed to know? Look, sweetheart, you wanna spend the night up here, that's fine with me, but I got a feeling your momma ain't gonna be too happy if you don't show up tonight."

"Oh, shit." I had forgotten all about going home.

"Nice language you're pickin' up." He brushed a strand of hair out of my eyes.

"Do you think she'll know about school and everything?"

"*Oh*, yeah. I'm sure she'll know about it."

"Oh, Case, what am I going to do? She'll kill me."

"Shoulda thought about that before. Come on, get your stuff. I'll give you a lift home."

As soon as we got in the car, I turned to him. "What do you think will happen to the dun?"

"Willya quit worryin' already? She can take care of herself."

"But why won't she come down, Case? She's not going back to Mooney's, is she?"

"I doubt it. She don't look too eager to go down no place."

"But how come? She's gotta go down someplace."

Casey shrugged.

"I'd take good care of her."

"*She* don't know that." Casey chuckled. "All she knows is this ain't her home."

"But then why doesn't she go back to Mooney's?"

" 'Cause maybe she don't like it over there. He don't take care of his birds. She's smart. She's gettin' out."

"So then why doesn't she come here?"

" 'Cause like I just told you, she's smart. She's too smart. She knows this ain't her home. She was born over there, not over here. Now, if she was dumb, maybe she'd come down."

"Very funny. Come on. What's she gonna do? She can't just fly forever."

"Nah ... she'll hang around for a while maybe. She'll go down someplace. She'll probably go lost over in the city or something. Not around here. Who knows? That's just like her nature or somethin', you know what I mean? That particular bird."

"But what if she doesn't come down? What if she doesn't find a good place to land?"

"What's the matter with you, you're talking crazy. Of course she'll go down, she'll find a place to land. This ain't exactly the Sahara Desert over here. She's gotta go down someplace. She just don't have no real home, that's all."

We didn't say anything the rest of the way back. When he pulled up in front of my house, I hesitated for a second, my fingers resting on the door handle. "Case?"

"What's the matter now?"

"Do you think maybe if I go up real early tomorrow morning I might catch the dun then, maybe?"

71

"I wouldn't count on it."

"I know, but I just mean *maybe*, if she's real tired or hungry or something."

"Sweetheart, she could be in Pennsylvania tomorrow for all I know. She didn't look like she was stickin' around to me."

"But just maybe, Case? I mean, if she's still here and everything?"

Casey turned away from me and tapped his fingers against the window. "Yeah. *May*be."

"Good." I unlocked the door and jumped out. "That's all I wanted to know."

But as things turned out, I didn't go up early the next morning. I didn't go up at all the next morning, or any other morning for a week. That was my punishment for skipping school. By the time I did get to the roof, around three o'clock, there was no trace of the silver dun. Neither Casey nor I ever saw her again.

9

FRANKIE'S ROOM WAS PANELED IN DARK WOOD, AND A rust-colored carpet covered most of the floor. In addition to a desk and dresser, he had a bookcase, an easy chair, and a set of display shelves in which he had arranged photographs, a mineral collection, and trophies from his junior high school softball team, of which he had been captain. On the wall directly over his bed, he had mounted Poppy's helmet and his shield.

I spent a lot of time in that room. As long as I was quiet, Frankie didn't mind if I sat in the chair and did my homework with him. Sometimes—when he and Michael brought "dates" back to the house—I even got paid to stay there. For twenty-five cents apiece, I wouldn't come out until the girls left.

I spent those evenings curled up in Frankie's bed, flipping through back issues of *Boy's Life* and seeing how many pieces of gum I could chew at one time. One night, not sure whether the girls had gone, I tiptoed into the kitchen and made myself a snack of crackers and grape jelly. The television was still on—I remember the shifting blue light from the living room—but the volume was low and I could detect a furtive quality in Frankie's voice that caught my attention. "She won't go for it," he said.

"Tell her you're gonna break up then," Michael urged. "I bet that'll work."

"I don't want to break up with her, Michael. We just started going out."

"I know, but you just gotta say that. Get her worried. Tell her that you're going nuts." Michael snickered. "Tell her that your nuts are going nuts!"

They started giggling.

"I'm so horny I could die!"

"Look at me," Michael said. "I'm stiff as a board."

"Yeah, but you can go over to Martha's house and get laid."

"Yeah? Well, so can you. I told you anytime you want, I just have to tell her you're my friend."

Frankie said something else, but his voice was so low I couldn't make it out. I heard one of them stand up and do something to his clothes.

"Now this is what Mr. Cunningham would have called erect," Michael said. His voice cracked on the last word and they burst out laughing. Mr. Cunningham was their gym teacher at Eli Whitney, and Michael was imitating him, exaggerating the Irish brogue of his speech. " 'When the male member is excited, it fills up with a rush of blood' "—he pronounced this word as though it rhymed with "should"—" 'and becomes erect. It is then ready for intercourse.' "

I stared down at the kitchen table and felt my face grow hot. I wasn't hungry anymore. I dumped the plate of crackers in

74

the trash and tried to duck back inside Frankie's room when Michael called, "Hey, Louie, is that you?"

"No, it's Mr. Cunningham!" The words popped out before I could think.

"You little sneak!" Frankie was up out of his chair in a flash. I ducked inside his room and locked the door just as he got there.

"Damn you, Louie, why can't you leave us alone just once? Go get some friends of your own and stop bugging me!"

"Take it easy, Frankie. Just calm down." Michael sounded amused. "It's no big deal. Just take it easy."

"She's supposed to stay in my room all night. That's the deal, Michael, that's why we pay her."

"Well your girlfriends left!" I cried. "I thought I could come out!"

Frankie kicked the door and I jumped back. I waited till they left, then climbed back onto Frankie's bed. I had the strangest feeling. I knew I had missed something, but I didn't know what it was. It was like listening to people speak a foreign language and then realizing that the words they used sounded just like the ones you used. But what did they *mean*? In the days that followed, I replayed that conversation a hundred times, searching for the key that would unlock its secret, but I never quite got it to make sense.

But as this mystery developed, another was soon solved. I had suspected that Frankie's recent enthusiasm for lifting weights was connected to his growing interest in girls. Although he was wiry and a good athlete, he wasn't big like Michael. I thought he was just trying to impress some girl, and would soon grow bored lifting bars up and down. It seemed so dumb. I told Frankie I was surprised at him.

75

Frankie's explanation was simple. It was just like flying pigeons, he said. If you weren't involved in it yourself, there was no way you could understand what it meant. It would be a waste of breath trying to explain. That was the end of the conversation.

Meanwhile, the intensity of their interest continued to grow. They spent every afternoon at the Greenpoint Y and every night at our house arguing over training strategies and planning their routines. They recorded every single workout in a spiral notebook: the name of the exercise, the number of sets, the amount of the weight, and the number of repetitions at each weight. I thought they were both nuts.

For Michael, in spite of the hard work, the whole thing was basically a lark. He strutted around our house bare chested, flexing his biceps and posing in front of the mirror. He could easily snatch me up and carry me over his head so I could touch the ceiling. I liked to do that. It was fun.

Frankie was different. He approached the whole project in deadly earnest. He never took his shirt off in front of me or paraded around the house. He wouldn't even let me stay in his room and watch while he did his sit-ups and push-ups each night. And he never boasted about his gains.

He didn't have to. Before long, I noticed the change. We had been arguing one night over who should get the last piece of a chocolate cake. Ready for a mock tussle, I tried to push Frankie away from the refrigerator. He didn't budge. I don't mean that he simply stayed put. I mean his whole body was planted on the spot, fixed, like a mountain or a tree or something that is not meant to be moved. He must have seen by my expression that I was shocked, for he managed a little half smile of complicity. That was the closest he ever came to showing off.

And then, accidentally, I discovered the deeper source of Frankie's interest. I had come home early one afternoon because of the snow, and I surprised Frankie and Michael poring over some papers on the kitchen table.

"Hi," I said. "What's that?"

Frankie covered the top of the page with his arm. "Nothing," he said.

"Hi," Michael said. "Go on, Frankie, let her see it."

"Michael!" It was the closest I had come to hearing my brother whine in a long time.

"Well, why not? What's the big deal? She's not your mom."

Frankie avoided my eyes, but he allowed Michael to pry the booklet from under his arm and slide it over to me. It was a copy of a previous examination for the fire department.

I blinked at Michael. "Are you thinking of joining?"

Frankie took a deep breath. "We both are." He went on before I had a chance to reply. "That's one reason we've been working out so hard. There's a physical, too, you know. It's tough. You gotta be in good shape."

He reached over for the book and flipped it open to a random page, which he began to study with great intensity.

I stared at the back of his head, then took off my coat and stomped the snow off my shoes. "You're gonna finish high school, aren't you?"

Frankie looked up. A flicker of relief crossed his face. "Of course I am. You can't even take the test till you're twenty-one."

"*Twenty-one?* Frankie, that's a long time. How do you know—"

"I *know*. Listen, Louie, please don't—"

I straightened up. "Don't worry," I said, annoyed that Frankie would underestimate me. I made an X over my heart. "I won't tell Ma."

10

I OPENED THE DOOR TO THE PET SHOP SLOWLY SO THAT
the kittens wouldn't run outside. The black one stumbled over
my sneaker as I squeezed through. The other two trotted out
from behind the counter, mewling up at me as they knocked
each other sideways trying to gain a foothold on my jeans. I
hauled the black one to my shoulder, and the two tigers rolled
over on the floor.

"Find any mice today?" I nuzzled the kitten with my chin.
"Hi, Joey."

"Hi, dolly." He took the cigarette out of his mouth and
pretended to be shocked. "There ain't no mice in here,
sweetheart. In *my* shop?"

I smiled back. The cat squirmed against my neck and I
scratched his ears. He flicked his tail back and forth, brushing
my cheek. I could feel the vibrations of his purring against my
collarbone.

"You guys want some food?" I knelt down to stroke the other two, letting them sink their translucent baby teeth into my fingers. With all three clinging to my clothes, I shuffled behind the counter and opened the small refrigerator that was wedged under the shelf. I wiped off a clump of feathers from the handle and pulled out a large, open can of cat food with a crusty spoon stuck inside. The black cat dug his claws into my back as he pivoted and jumped down. "All right, all right. Just let me get this on the plate." I scooped out a chunk and dumped it in their dish. A glance through the glass counter assured me that Joey wasn't looking; I quickly poured out some milk and mashed it in. I wiped my hands on the seat of my pants and looked over at the table where Joey and a man named Nicky were playing cards. I didn't like Nicky. His face was pink and fleshy, and he wore a diamond ring on his baby finger. Hector had told me he was married to one of the Rockettes and had been arrested once for some kind of gambling operation. He was supposed to have one of the fanciest roofs in the whole city. They said he'd even carpeted his shanty.

I headed for the back room. "Should I just feed the birds or what, Joey? Hi, Nicky."

Nicky grunted without looking up.

"Sure," said Joey. "Go feed 'em, give 'em all a drink."

Nicky discarded an eight of spades but held on to the edge of it. "I caught one of Casey's birds yesterday." He snapped the corner of the card as he let go. "A strawberry cock."

"I know." I waited, thinking he had more to say.

"Gimme a buck, you can have him back."

"Catch-keep." I shrugged. "We never buy them back. You know that." I disappeared into the back room, where the large coops were waiting to be cleaned. The wall separating the two

79

ends of the shop had been put up years ago, one night when
everyone was drunk—at least, that's what Casey told me, and I
believed it. There were holes punched all the way through,
and if you sat in the right spot, near the coop, you had a clear
view of the round table. Even with the door closed, you could
hear everything. I pressed myself into the corner and watched
them play for a while. They didn't say much. Then Joey
grabbed a card and threw down something from his hand.
"Gin!" he cried. "Hah! Lemme see what you got."

Nicky deliberately laid all his cards face down and rubbed his
nose. "This ain't no place for a girl, Joey. I been telling you
that all along."

"Lemme see your hand already." Joey reached across the table
and turned over the cards. "Ooooh, boy, you're gettin' beat
today!"

"It ain't right," Nicky went on. "This here's for pigeon-flyers."

"She's a good pigeon-flyer. She's good with the birds." Joey
wetted the end of the pencil with his tongue and jotted down
their scores. "She don't bother nobody."

"You don't think there's something funny about it? Her
going up on Casey's roof like that?"

"What do you mean, 'funny'?" Joey frowned. "Come on. You
want me to beat you three out of five or what?"

The front door creaked open and Tommy Parelli strolled in.
He was the only pigeon-flyer I knew who always looked as if
he'd just stepped out of a bath.

"Hey, watch the cats!" Joey called out as all three kittens
raced for the door.

Tommy stuck out a patent leather loafer and batted them
away.

"Why don't you put up a screen or something?" He nodded

over at Nicky, who had picked up the deck and started shuffling again.

"Well, Mr. Parelli!" Joey boomed. "Come on over and join the card game."

"No, I can't." He hoisted himself carefully onto the metal stool at Nicky's left, tugging gently at each trouser leg as he shifted his position. "I gotta pick up my kid in a few minutes, take him shopping. He wants one of them leather jackets— what do you call them, bomber jackets? I promised I'd take him over there today."

"Where you gonna take him?"

"I dunno. Shepherd's, I guess. Out by Flatbush."

"They supposed to have them there?"

Tommy shrugged. "That's what he says. His friends all got them over there."

"They're expensive," Joey said. "Why don't you take him over by Olympia, out in Forest Hills? You remember Heshie, with the show pigeons? Heshie's father-in-law works there, maybe he can give you a break."

"Yeah? Last time you sent someone over there, he gave them a break and got stiffed with a rubber check. That was your boy Casey. You don't remember that?"

Joey turned back to his cards. "Yeah," he muttered. "I forgot about that. But they got it all straightened out, right? He paid him up and everything."

Nicky leaned back in his chair. "What's he buying leather jackets for? He can't even feed his birds. He's lucky if he feeds his kids."

"Aw, what are you talking about? That was last year already." Joey glanced over towards the back room, but I knew he couldn't see me. "Come on, you guys want coffee? I'm going across the street, I'll get you coffee."

"The girl's here," Nicky said. "Why don't you send the girl?"

I hated when they called me that, as if I didn't have a name.

"The girl's here?" Tommy sounded surprised. "Where is she, in the back?"

"Yeah," Nicky answered. "That's why he don't want you talking about Casey."

"I'll talk about whoever I damn please! Where the hell you think this is, Russia?"

"So who told you not to talk? Did anybody tell you not to talk?" Joey asked. "What do you listen to him for anyway?" He turned to Nicky. "What's the matter with you?"

"Nothing. That creep Casey owes money all over this fucking town. He even borrows from his girlfriend."

"Don't talk about girlfriends, Nicky."

"Aw, shut up, Joey. He's taking money from his girlfriend and you know it. He owes you money, too, don't he? I hear he's back with Ray again anyway, picking up change in the stolen car business. And other things."

"What do you care? Does he owe *you* money? Then don't worry about it."

Nicky looked up at Tommy, who was intent on brushing a speck of lint off his jacket. "Henry told me they ain't sellin' him *nothin'* by Jackson's anymore. Cash on the line, that's the only way he walks outta there with *shit*. He owes Jackson over two hundred bucks. Can you believe that? I heard that Fingers went in one night for a sack of feed while they was still partners. Henry was over there, he said Fingers didn't even know. His own partner! Tried to walk out of there with two sacks of corn and Jackson stopped him. Fingers hit the ceiling.

Henry said he started hollering, 'I been flyin' pigeons here my whole life and I ain't never took *nothin'* I didn't pay for.' But Jackson told him, from now on, Casey's roof is strictly cash on the line, he don't care *who* comes in for it."

"So what did he do?" Tommy asked. "He pay for it or what?"

"*Hell* no. Are you kidding? He walked outta there. He's never set foot inside Jackson's since then, and that's too bad, you know, cause Fingers is okay. He's all right."

Joey pulled out a sad-looking pack of cigarettes from his shirt pocket and tapped one out.

"Lemme have one of them, huh, Joe?"

"Why don't you buy your own cigarettes?" Tommy asked. "You're always bummin' off everybody else. You got a ton of money and you never spring for nothing."

"What do you mean?" Nicky whined. "Anyway, Joey don't mind, do you, Joe?"

Joey stuck the pack back inside his shirt and pulled the edges of his button-down sweater tight across his chest. "As a matter of fact . . ." He winked at Tommy, then stretched his hand for the matches and lit up.

"Well, you asked him!" Tommy laughed and got up from the stool.

"Come *on*." Nicky stuck his hand out and snapped his fingers.

Joey dragged it out a few more seconds before tossing the pack across the table. He pushed his chair back and stood up.

"You want me to buy you a pack?"

"Where you going?"

"Just across the street. I told you, I'm going for coffee. You gonna be here?"

"Yeah. Here." He dug in his pocket for some change. "Black. Extra sugar."

"You sure you don't want no cigarettes?"

"Nah, I'll get 'em on the way home."

Joey turned to Tommy. "You want coffee?"

He shook his head. "I'm going out with you. I gotta pick up my kid." He stopped at one of the cages near the front door. "Where'd you get these Homers, Joe?"

"They came in yesterday from the Bronx. Mike brought them in."

"How much you want for 'em?" Tommy unlatched the hook and reached in for the cock. He spread the left wing and inspected the feathers.

"Fifteen for the pair."

"They're good, huh?" Tommy let go of the wing and stroked the tail feathers. Then he examined each foot, the beak, and both eyes. He handed the cock to Joey and reached in for the hen. He repeated the procedure, taking his time. He looked over at Joey. "Wrap 'em up," he said.

Joey stepped behind the counter and reached up to the second shelf for a brown paper bag. He lowered the cock inside, then took the hen and placed her next to him. There was a slight rustle as the pair adjusted to the dark. Joey folded the top of the bag over three or four times, smoothing each fold before making the next. He stapled the bag closed. "Here you go." He pinched the sides of the bag together just above where the birds' heads were and tore a little hole in it. He tore another hole a few inches farther up, then turned the bag around and did the same thing on the other side.

Tommy pulled out his wallet and withdrew two bills, which Joey slipped into a metal cash tray under the counter. When

Tommy picked up the sack by the top fold, the birds' feet skittered against the stiff paper.

Joey turned to Nicky. "Okay, take care of the customers. I'll be back in a couple of minutes."

Nicky stuck the cigarette in his mouth and shuffled the deck one more time. He laid out a neat row of seven cards and began a round of solitaire. I went back to work. Before five minutes had passed, the door banged open again and Hector burst in. He was trying to pull his sweatshirt off over his head, but it was stuck, and his long fingers were plucking uselessly at the hem.

"Hey!" he cried. "Who turned off the lights?"

Nicky looked up, picked at his nose, and went back to his cards.

"Anybody home?" Hector twirled around, the faded green cotton completely obliterating his face. "Where am I? Get me outta here!"

"All right, cut it out." Nicky ground his cigarette out in the ashtray.

"No. I'm stuck, man. Really. I ain't kidding." He tore at his sleeves as he staggered around the room.

I poked my head out the door to get a better look and burst out laughing. "Hey, Hector, is that you? Who's in there with you?"

He turned in my direction. "Who's that? Who's got that funny little voice?"

"What's the matter, Hector? Your head swell up or something, can't get your clothes off?" I laughed again. "Caught too many pigeons, huh? Got a big head. You caught a couple of our birds last week, now you think you're really something!" I grabbed for one of the flailing arms and missed. "Okay, okay, just hold on." I stepped out where I had more room.

"Come on, man, help me. I'll die in here. I can't breathe. Aaaaggghh!" He fell to one knee, gasping for breath.

"You're crazy." I tapped his head. "Hold still a minute."

"Hurry, before I die in here!"

"Just shut up." I slipped my fingers inside the collar of the sweatshirt, stretched it open, and tugged it over his head.

"Aaaaaahh!" He collapsed on the floor, then immediately recovered, grabbed my hand, and pretended to cover it with kisses.

"Yuck! Stop it!" I pulled away, snatched the sweatshirt from the floor, and wiped my hand on it.

Hector laughed. "What's the matter with you? You know how many girls out there would die for me to kiss their hand?"

"Yeah. None." I raised my eyebrows and tossed the sweatshirt back at him. "They'd all die *after* you kissed them!"

"Think you're pretty funny, huh? Just wait a few years," he teased. "You gonna change your mind about kissing."

"Not me," I boasted.

Hector stood up and dusted off his pants. "Man, you still a baby." He smoothed his wispy mustache and grinned. "Wait till you be seventeen."

"So? Seventeen's not so old."

"Well, it's a lot older than whatever *you* got."

"So big deal." I glanced over at the table. Nicky immediately looked back down at his cards. "Come on in the back, I'm feeding the birds."

Hector started after me, but paused for a minute at the table. "So how's it goin', man?" He took out a pack of cigarettes and offered them to Nicky. Nicky ignored him. Hector lit one up. "So where's Joe?"

Nicky turned over a card. "He's out."

"I can see that, man."

"So why'd you ask?"

Hector sucked in his breath but didn't say anything. His fingers were on the doorknob when Nicky spoke.

"Just keep your hands off her, that's all."

Hector turned around very slowly and leaned over the table. "What did you say?"

"Come on, Hector, forget it." I pulled at his arm.

Nicky continued to stare at the cards.

Just then Joey returned, carrying a brown sack that was leaking from the bottom.

"Hiya, Hector. What's up?"

Hector leaned closer to Nicky, who refused to look at him. "I'm askin' you, just what the hell is that supposed to mean?"

"Aw, what's going on now?" Joey set the bag down on the table. "What's the matter with you two this time? I can't leave the store for five minutes without—"

"What the hell do you mean?" Hector shouted. "Answer me!"

Nicky looked directly at Joey. "It's your fault, Joey. I told you not to let the girl in here. She's only makin' trouble."

"I am not! I didn't do anything, Joey! It's him!"

"What are you talking about?" Joey demanded. "Hector, what's going on?"

"Man, this motherfucker shooting off his mouth telling me keep my hands off her! I ain't done nothing!"

"Hector, Hector, take it easy. Watch that language here."

Hector looked at me. "Sorry."

"Oh, Joey, stop it! Hector can talk however he wants!"

"All right, all of you, calm down. Just ignore him, Hector. He's just trying to bust your chops."

"Man, you better watch your mouth." Joey stuck his arm out as Hector jerked towards Nicky again. " 'Cause I'm getting sick of you, man, understand? I mean it, Nicky, don't mess with me no more." As he turned away from the table, his knee accidentally bumped one of the metal folding chairs. Without saying another word, he yanked the chair out from under the table and slammed it down on the floor a few feet away. The kittens flew behind the counter. Hector stormed out of the shop.

Shaking his head, Joey picked up the chair and sat down. He opened the paper sack and set three containers on the stained Formica top. Each formed a little puddle underneath.

"Here. I brought you coffee."

I took one of the cups but remained standing. Joey turned to Nicky. "What do you always give them such a hard time for?"

Nicky tore open two sugars and dumped them in his coffee.

"Yeah," I piped up. "What do you always give us such a hard time for? We never bother you."

Joey looked over at me. "Don't worry, baby. He don't mean nothing personal. He just likes to give them a hard time. He don't really mean nothing, he just don't know when to keep his mouth shut, that's all."

"No, you're wrong, Joey. I don't like that particular kid. I don't like them Spics starting to come in here, and that kid in particular seems a little too much at home. Especially with the girl."

"He's my friend, Nicky! And anyway, it's none of your business."

"It's okay, dolly, relax. You know this guy, he likes to break horns. It was nothing."

We sipped our coffee in silence. The gurgling of the pigeons filled the room. Joey tipped his chair back and peeled the cellophane off a new pack of Camels. The black kitten ventured out from under the counter. He crept over to me and meowed, but I ignored him. When I finished my coffee, I stuffed the cup into the trash and shifted from one foot to the other, waiting for somebody to say something. When no one did, I retreated to the back room, leaving the door open.

After a minute, I heard Nicky scrape up the cards and start shuffling. "He had his hands all over her, Joey. You know what I'm saying? Kissing her and everything. It makes me sick."

I started back to protest, but Joey stuck out his foot and kicked the door shut in my face. It slammed so hard it banged part way open again.

"What's the matter with you?" he hissed. "They play around. Leave 'em alone, Nicky. They ain't doin' nothing wrong."

"There's gonna be trouble with her one of these days, Joey. I'm tellin' you. She don't belong here. And them Spics don't belong here neither. Let 'em stay over on the other side, with the goddamn niggers."

"You wanna play cards or run for mayor?" Joey reached for the deck, but Nicky covered it with his hand.

"I'm tellin' you, Joe."

"Come on already. Deal the cards."

They started another round of gin. I went back to the big coop, opened it, then slammed it shut. The noise set off a flurry among the pigeons. "I didn't do anything!" I scowled at them, but there was a quiver in my voice. Casey had told me a hundred times not to let guys like Nicky bother me. Nicky was an ignorant son of a bitch and a lousy flyer. But everything Nicky said was a lie. Hector was my friend, that was all. He'd never done anything bad to me. It was all lies. It was lies about Casey, too. Maybe Casey borrowed money sometimes, but he always paid it back. Casey didn't have a girlfriend either; he was married. And I wasn't the one who caused the trouble. It was Nicky who made everything ugly, not me. The longer I stared at the birds, the angrier I got, until I couldn't stand it anymore. I stormed back in and faced Nicky across the table.

"I didn't do anything wrong and you know it!"

He refused to look up.

"Of course you didn't, dolly." Joey eyed us back and forth.

"I said I didn't do anything wrong, Nicky!"

Nicky scraped an imaginary speck off the back of a card, but he still wouldn't look at me. I grabbed the edge of the table with both hands, jerked it up, and then slammed it back down. The cards went flying.

Nicky looked at me then, and his mouth hung open.

"You're a liar," I said.

Nicky didn't move. Even Joey remained glued to his chair. Suddenly I felt much calmer.

"I can't feed the birds tonight, Joey. I have to go."

I opened the front door and took a few deep breaths. From out of nowhere, the black kitten darted past me onto the sidewalk.

"Come back!" I cried. "Come back here right now!"

But the kitten bounced off down the block. It didn't pay any attention to what I said.

11

THE MAN WITH THE LEATHER JACKET HAD SHOWN UP on the roof again, and Casey had sent me away. I dragged my feet as far as Grand Street, where Angelo had his coop, then hurried across two blocks and down to South Fifth. I yelled up to Hector from the street, and after a few seconds he appeared at the edge of the roof and waved.

When I got up there, I was surprised to find him sitting on a crate, hands hanging limp between his knees. His birds were preening on top of the coop. "What's the matter, Hector?"

"Nothing."

"Don't you feel good?"

He looked up. "I'm okay. What's up?"

"Nothing. I got kicked off so Casey could talk to his gangster friend."

"Who's that?"

"I don't know. You don't know those guys, do you?"

"I know some. What did he look like ?"

"I don't know. Kind of pudgy. Black hair, all slicked back. Shiny shoes. He wears this leather jacket, not like a motorcycle jacket, more like a sports coat sort of. Very neat." I made a face. "You know who it is?"

"Yeah. I know. I'm pretty sure anyway."

I shrugged. "He didn't look very tough to me."

Hector shook his head. "It's got nothing to do with that. That's just in the movies."

"Well, he looked kind of dumb to me. And he's not very nice. He never even looks at me. Every time he comes up, Casey sends me away. I don't see why I couldn't just stay and fly the birds. I wouldn't bother them."

"He comes up a lot?"

"Well, no, not really. This is only the second time since I've been there. Why?"

"Nothing. I was just wondering. You think Casey would do me a favor?"

"I guess so. If it's not money."

Hector dusted off the seat of his pants and reached for the pole. "You know something, Shorty?" He banged on the coop and the pigeons swooped off over the bridge. "Someday I'm gonna be rich like them guys, too, you know that?"

I laughed. "Not the way you fly pigeons!"

"Yeah? I ain't talking about pigeons. You'll see, and then I'll have a real stock, hundreds of birds, like Casey, or Fingers, then I can really fly. You can't do much with a little stock like this. I'll have my own house and I'll put them up there. No more shit like this stinking roof."

"You gonna carpet it like Nicky? And hire a guard?"

He stuck his hands in his back pockets and looked around.

"Hector?"

"Huh?"

"I was just joking. How're you gonna get so rich?"

"I don't know. I just know I ain't moppin' offices like my old man. What time does Casey get up there usually?"

"About four, four-thirty. Why?"

He shrugged.

"Well, I can tell you one thing, Casey's not gonna give you money. He never has money. We even have to get credit at Joey's half the time." The words hung in the air for only a second before I realized what I had done. "Hector, listen, I didn't mean to say that, okay? Please don't tell anyone I said that. It's only a little credit, it's nobody's business. Really."

"Take it easy, Shorty. Everybody knows about Casey."

"What do you mean? What about him?"

"Relax! Everybody knows he's got credit. It's no big deal. He owes money everywhere."

"He does not! Who told you that, Nicky?"

"No, not Nicky."

"Well, I hope you don't listen to Nicky. He's just jealous 'cause Casey's a better flyer than he'll ever be."

"Believe me, I don't listen to Nicky. I just know. Everybody knows."

"Well, it's not true."

Hector didn't answer.

"Anyway, Nicky never liked Casey in the first place. In case you haven't noticed, Casey won't even talk to him."

"Look, just forget it, okay?"

"Well, I don't want you spreading stories that aren't even true."

Hector wheeled around. "Listen, Shorty, in the first place I don't spread stories about anybody, and in the second place, don't tell me what's true. You don't know nothing about it."

"I do, too! What's that supposed to mean?"

"Aw, forget it, Shorty. Why'd you come up here anyway?"

"I told you, I got kicked off over there. I thought you might like some company."

"How come you only come up here when you get kicked off over there?"

"Hector, that's not fair! I come here, but I chase for Casey. I have to be there every day."

"I know, I know. I don't blame you." He slapped at his coop. It was hard to tell what he was thinking.

"You have nice birds, though. Really. They're still talking about your Homer."

Hector smiled, but it wasn't a real smile. "Yeah. Well, let's fly them, okay?"

We stopped talking and concentrated on the stock. They flew really tight for such a small bunch. We watched as his birds mixed in with a bundle from Angelo's, but the wind died and they all just drifted together for a while. Before long, Hector's birds were surrounded by the larger stock. They didn't go too far, and soon Hector began whistling a soft, *chirrup-y* sort of sound to signal his birds back down. Little by little, most of them managed to weave their way out of the crowd and head for home. It was a clear day, and a dozen flyers in that neighborhood were on their rooftops, waiting for the ones that didn't make it.

Christmas that year was a disaster. My big present was a wool parka. It was green, my favorite color, but my only comment—

aimed in Junior's direction—was that it didn't look much like
a door to me. Ma snatched the coat away and said if that was
my attitude, maybe I didn't deserve anything at all. Junior
surprised me by staying calm. He handed me back the coat, then
turned and put his arms around my mother. He told her not
to worry, everything would work out. I said I was sorry three
times, but Ma ignored me. She asked Junior to take her for a
walk. When they left, Frankie thanked me for spoiling Christmas and slammed the door to his room. I sat on the floor next
to the tree and ate every piece of candy I could find. Then I felt
sick.

We had midday dinner with Junior's brother and sister-in-law
out in Queens. Their kids were babies, and since Frankie
wasn't speaking to me, I didn't say ten words all afternoon. As
soon as we got back, I changed clothes and ran over to the
roof. Casey was drinking wine and chasing the birds.

"I beat you," he scowled. "I been up here since ten o'clock
this morning. *Ten o' clock!* You hear me?" He took a long sip
from the bottle and heaved it against the trash. "Merry
Christmas."

12

It got cold right after New Year's and stayed that way all month. I kept a pair of jeans on the roof, and Casey had collected enough warm clothes up there to open a store. I especially liked wearing his sweatshirts. They reached down to my knees, and the sleeves were so long they had to be rolled halfway back. One afternoon, Casey saw me pulling one on and motioned me over to the shanty. "Why do you wear these old rags in the first place?" he asked. "They're bigger than you are."

"I like them."

He started folding back the sleeves for me. "Look at you. Your nose is already bright red and you just got up here. What are you gonna do all afternoon?"

"I'm not cold. Really."

"I got you coffee."

"Thanks. Hey!" I suddenly realized it was a weekday. "What are you doing up here anyway?"

"What am I doing up here? Sweetheart, it's my roof, remember?"

"You know what I mean. How come you're not working?"

"What are you, the I.R.S? Don't worry about it."

"Casey, you didn't get fired, did you?"

"Aw, Louie, relax. I took the afternoon off, okay?"

I blew into my cup and let the steam warm my face.

"I got you something else, too." He had a funny look on his face.

He pointed to the end of the counter. There was a brown paper sack half hidden behind the hot plate. "Look in that bag."

The top was carefully folded over itself a few times and there were two slits in the sides. I wondered why Casey would make such a big deal over a new bird. He brought pigeons up to the roof all the time.

The bird jumped as I reached in, but I pinned it against the shelf and then used my left hand to steer it out of the sack. One wing got free and started flapping wildly till I managed to press the bird against my stomach and smooth the wing into place.

"She's beautiful, Case." It was a silver dun, a little hen, sleek and clean with clear eyes. "She looks young."

"Yeah. She's about a year old. Your age." He grinned.

"Very funny. Where'd you get her?"

Casey took another gulp of coffee. He had an asbestos throat; he could drink anything right off the boil. "She's for you. You took it so hard about losing that silver dun a while back, I thought you'd like this."

"I love her, Case, she's beautiful." Casey was plucking at a thread in his jeans. It occurred to me that he felt shy about

97

giving me a gift. I pulled out one wing and examined the tips. All ten primaries were in perfect shape. "She looks like a good flying bird."

Casey nodded. "She ought to be good. But she's yours, babe. You don't gotta mix her in with the stock. I thought you might like to keep her home for a pet."

"But Case! She's a Flight, she's not a show bird."

"Yeah, but you're entitled to a pet, if you want it. I gave her to you. You can do whatever you want with her. It's up to you. I just know how much you love them silver duns."

"I do, Case. Thank you." I went over and gave him a quick hug. "I want to mix her in with the regular stock, though. That's where she belongs, so she can fly with them. She can still be special, right?"

Casey shrugged. "Not really, babe. You want to mix her in, that's fine, but you can't control what happens then. You gonna worry or start holding back the rest of the stock 'cause you're nervous about one particular bird? You get to be a mutt real quick that way."

"Case! Have I ever done that? Have I ever been a mutt?" I turned away from him and stroked the little dun, who was beginning to calm down.

"Did I say that? You ain't listening to me. I said you don't *wanna* be a mutt."

"Well, I won't be. I can mix her in and still let her be special."

"Yeah? And what happens if she gets caught? We got catch-keep with everybody."

"I know, Case." The dun's throat vibrated against my hand.

"You ain't gonna go beggin'—'Just this once, please, gimme my bird back?'—like Nicky and them guys do?"

"Casey, have I ever done that?"

"No, but that's what I'm saying. They all gotta be the same here. If you want her to fly with the stock, then she's got to be treated just like all the other birds."

"But, Case, I can treat her like everybody else and just *feel* special about her, right? 'Cause you gave her to me and she's really my bird. Not that I'll treat her any better," I added quickly. "You know I treat all the birds good."

"You better, or I wouldn't let you up here."

"I will, Case. I always have."

"Okay. You do like you please. It's just a present. I thought you'd like it."

"I do. I love her. I'm gonna mix her in and I bet she'll be one of our best flyers. Next spring we can breed from her. We'll start a whole new line of silver duns."

"You're getting a little ahead of yourself, aren't you? What if she don't mix in with the stock and goes lost?"

I turned away and kissed the top of the bird's head. "So what?" I lied. "She goes lost. I lost a lot of birds before."

"Okay, boss, whatever you say. Go throw her in the screen now. I already fed them."

I snuggled the bird in the crook of my arm, unlatched the shanty door and then latched it again from the outside. "Don't worry," I murmured to the hen as I walked her over to the coop. "You are special, no matter what Casey says. Just fly good and don't go lost, okay? I'll take good care of you." I nuzzled the back of her neck with my cheek. "I promise." Then I tossed her inside with the rest of the stock.

13

I WAS SWEEPING THE FLOOR OF THE PET SHOP WHEN Hector burst through the door dragging a wooden carrier full of pigeons.

"Hey, Shorty, look at what I got!" He reached into the cage, grabbed a white Homer, and flourished it over his head. "You know who this belongs to?"

I shook my head. "Butchie the Old Man?"

"Unh-unh. Guess again."

I put down the broom and went over to examine the bird. Since I didn't keep track of the Homer guys, the single yellow band didn't mean anything to me. "Tito's the only guy I know with all-white Homers. Whose is it?"

"This comes all the way from Bensonhurst, man. It's one of Ray's birds, can you dig that?"

"Who's Ray?"

"Who's Ray? What's the matter with you, Shorty? Don't

Casey ever tell you nothing? Ray. Ray Tertullo. He practically owns this whole neighborhood."

"What's that got to do with Casey?"

"Nothing," Joey broke in.

Hector looked over at him. "She knows, man, Ray's been up there on the roof."

"Hector, do me a favor, huh?"

"All right, whatever you say, man. Anyway, what's the difference? I'm gonna take advantage of this bird."

"What do you mean?"

"I'm gonna return it in person, see, as a favor, and I'm gonna ask him for a job. Casey's supposed to tell him about me. He said he would."

"What kind of job, Hector? You can't do anything."

"That's what you think. I can drive, girl. I'm going to make deliveries. Run errands. That kind of stuff."

"You got a license?"

"Shit, they don't care about that."

"Well, what are you going to deliver? Pigeons?" I'd never heard of anyone delivering pigeons.

"No, Shorty. Things you don't know nothing about. Ask Casey. He'll explain it to you."

"Hector, cool it." Joey flashed him a warning look.

"I just meant that him and Ray used to be kind of tight, you know. They still do a few things together."

"Aw, you don't know what you're talking about." Joey stuck a cigarette in his mouth, but he didn't light it. "How'd you end up with one of his birds anyway?"

"I don't know. Must of gone lost."

"Lemme see." Joey tugged at the bird's foot and studied the

bands. "Yeah, that's Ray's all right. Take it back. I bet he'll give you five bucks for making the trip."

"Five bucks, man? I don't give a shit about five bucks, I want a job. What do you think, Joey? You think he'll give me a chance?"

"Hector, in the first place, they don't go outside for help very often. What do you want to start with them for anyway? Do yourself a favor and forget about working for them guys, you hear me?"

Hector ignored him. "I gotta go. See you later." He grabbed his carrier and left just as Fingers walked in carrying coffee. "Hiya, Louie, Joe."

"Hi, Fingers." I continued sweeping while the two of them sat down at the table and opened the steaming containers.

"I got for you, too, Louie. How's business, Joe?"

"Not too bad. How's everything by you?"

"Okay. Can't complain. My cousin brought in a couple hundred birds last week. Old man Berger retired, you know. He's moving to Florida, sold his whole stock. My cousin brought them over to my roof last night. What a mess. My wife's having a fit." Fingers laughed. "It's the only thing ever made her wish I was back with Casey!" He took a sip of coffee and turned to me. "How's that little silver dun?"

"The what? The dun? You mean, the new one?"

"Yeah," he chuckled. "What one did you think I meant? I thought you'd like her. I remember you telling Joey once they was your favorites."

I stopped pushing the broom. I hadn't told anyone about Casey giving me the dun.

"I picked her up in Canarsie, from a chuck-up with Danny Bonello, he's a kid flies out there, about fifteen, sixteen years old. We got catch-keep, but I don't even want her in the neighborhood 'cause I want to teach this kid a lesson. I was gonna ship her up to the Bronx, in fact, when Casey stops by the other night on a little business." He raised his eyebrows at Joey, who nodded.

"That's good. He's all squared away now?"

"With me he is." Fingers turned back to me. "I didn't know when I'd see you, so I gave him the silver dun and told him to give it to you."

I gripped the back of the empty chair and lowered myself into it by degrees. "Oh. Yeah. I meant to thank you when you came in. I just forgot. I'm sorry."

"You don't gotta thank me, sweetheart. I just wanted to know you got her okay."

"Oh, I did, Fingers. And I really like her. Really. She's beautiful. Thanks." I stood up. "Here, Joey, you want the rest of my coffee? I can't finish it." I held out the unopened container and refused to acknowledge his puzzled look.

"No, dolly, I still got mine."

I carried the cup to the back room and poured it down the sink. "I gotta finish up in here," I called back. "I'll see you later." I paused. "And, Fingers, thanks again."

I entered the large coop and sank to the middle of the floor. The pigeons fluttered down from their posts, plumping their feathers as they rearranged themselves on the concrete. They surged back and forth in waves, surrounding me, begging for their dinner. They clucked and cooed insistently, but a long time passed before I got up from the floor to fetch their feed.

14

Six mornings a week Junior was showered, shaved, and out the door by a quarter to seven. Sunday was the only day he slept in. Then, I got to be the first one up. I liked waking to a house so quiet you could hear the walls creak and the refrigerator hum. I nestled under the covers a few minutes longer, enjoying the stillness. On this particular Sunday, even the noise from the street seemed unusually muffled, and as soon as I looked out the window I knew why. It was snowing; it must have snowed all night. Huge drifts had piled up against the cars. The air was blurred with thick, soft flakes. It was beautiful, but I couldn't help feeling slightly disappointed. You couldn't fly the pigeons in the middle of a snowstorm, and no flying meant no Casey. He wouldn't bother to come up.

Still, I had to feed the birds, no matter what. I pulled on my overalls and a sweater and proceeded into the kitchen. I fixed myself a bowl of raisin bran and ate it standing at the sink, staring out the window. Next door, the neatly fenced-off patch of Mr. Laskowski's garden was a sheet of solid white. Around its edges, the shiny black skeletons of bushes waved aimlessly back and forth, covered in furry snow. Mr. Laskowski's forsythias would someday burst into gold again, and the dense, ruffled squash plants would reappear, and the tall leafy stalks of tomatoes. Even the bare mimosa at the far end of his yard would be dappled with rose and coral blooms. But that would not be until summer, and in the middle of February, when the whole world was white and cold and still, summer seemed impossible. I rinsed out my bowl and headed for the roof.

Nearly blinded by the snow, I ploughed across McCarren Park, chin tucked into my coat, my hand clutching the hood so it wouldn't blow off my head. By the time I reached the Russian Church I was exhausted. I leaned up against the gate to catch my breath, then pushed on the last few blocks.

My fingers were freezing as I unlocked the door on North Eighth. I climbed the stairs slowly, shivering with every step. All of a sudden, as I reached the sixth-floor landing, I stiffened and drew back. The door to the roof was open. Heart pounding, I pulled myself up the last few steps, trying not to make a sound. There was no sign that the door had been forced. Cautiously, I looked around. The birds were milling about inside the screen. There were footprints everywhere. Someone moved inside the shanty and I froze. Then I saw that it was Casey, and he was laughing at me. I stumbled across the roof. "Hey! I didn't think you'd be here!" I pounded him on the arm.

"Hey yourself. Here." Casey held out an old green beach towel. "Stop hitting me and dry yourself off. You'll have some coffee and warm up."

105

"I didn't think you'd come out in this weather." I saw that he had already put water on the hot plate.

"Yeah? I brought up doughnuts and everything."

The Sunday papers were spread out. I felt so happy just to have him there. Then I saw the six pack of beer. Two bottles were already missing. Some of the glow disappeared, and I remembered I hadn't seen Casey for several days, not since my last trip to the pet store. I took off my gloves and rubbed my hands over the pot of water. "Did you feed the birds already?"

"What do you think?"

"Yeah."

"I knew you were smart."

"Did you fix that leak in the coop?"

"Nah, don't worry about it. I'll get it next week."

"Casey, don't you think it's gonna be wet for them like this?

"Louie, don't get on my case, okay? I told you I'd fix it."

"Okay. I was just asking."

"Well I'm just telling you."

"Okay!" I grabbed a jelly doughnut and wolfed it down. I finished a second and was biting into a third when I changed my mind and set it down. I had resolved not to do this, but now some stubbornness in me took over. I cleared my throat. "Casey . . ." I began.

Casey lowered the paper and looked me. "Well, what do you want now?"

I looked out the window. "Case, you know the silver dun you gave me?"

"What about it?"

"Where'd you get it from?"

He picked up the paper again and searched for his place.

"How do I remember? One of the stores. How many places can you get a Flight?"

I stared at the fold in the newspaper. "Fingers told me he gave it to you to give to me."

"Yeah? Well, Fingers is a liar."

"I'm just saying what he told me."

"And I'm just telling you he's a liar. Why would he give you a bird?"

"He's my friend."

"Bullshit. He don't even hardly know you. What's with you? You think because somebody talks to you they're your friend?"

"Well then why would he say it if it's not true?"

"Louie, are you calling me a liar?"

"No, but I just don't understand why he would have said that. I didn't ask him or anything."

"Maybe I picked it up from him. I told you, I don't even remember. Don't make such a big deal out of it."

"But, Case, it *is* a big deal. You said you got it for me."

"Louie, look. If you're gonna nag me all day, just go home, all right? I don't need it. I came up here to get away from it, you understand? This is the one place nobody can get to me. I don't know what's the matter with you. I gave you the damn bird. If you don't want it, fine, go break its fucking neck. Jesus Christ. You know something? I was looking forward to seeing you today. I really was. You're the one person I thought I could see and no hassles. I brought you doughnuts, I got the paper. I'm trying to be nice to you, and now you want a piece of my ass too. You're just like everybody else."

"I am not!"

"Well, then don't act like them. Now sit down already. You ain't going nowhere. Here." He shoved the funny papers at me. I took them without meeting his eyes. He made room for me on the bench and I sat down on the edge, as far away from him as I could get.

"Hand me one of them doughnuts, willya? And grab me a couple of aspirins while you're at it, I got a headache you wouldn't believe."

I got up and handed him the aspirin, which he swallowed with his beer. It served him right that his head hurt. He had lied to me about the bird. And I was *not* like everybody else. I thumbed through the doughnuts and gave him one that had coconut sprinkled all over it. I hated coconut.

I sat back down and snapped open the comics so hard I ripped the page.

"Now don't go getting an attitude."

"I don't have an attitude."

"Yes you do. Something's bothering you again, I can tell."

I didn't answer.

"Go on. What is it this time?"

"Nothing."

"Nothing. She's in a snit about nothing."

"I am not! I just wish you didn't have to drink all the time, that's all." I flipped through the comics without seeing a thing, then picked up another section.

"Yeah? Well you know what I wish? I wish you wouldn't get on my back about everything, okay? I had a few beers, that's all. What's the big deal? Everything's a big deal with you."

I snatched my cup down from the shelf and wiped it out with a paper towel. "You want coffee?"

"No, I don't want coffee. You listen to me, Louie. You don't know what you're talking about. I felt like having a few beers. It don't mean nothing. I can stop drinking anytime I want. A few drinks don't mean nothing, that's what you don't understand."

"I understand."

"Yeah. Well." He lay back on the bench. "I'm just wiped out, that's all. It ain't the booze, Louie, it's this headache that's killing me. Just let me rest for half an hour, okay, sweetheart? I had a bad night if you want to know the truth. I'll be okay soon's this headache goes away. Okay?"

I nodded, but his eyes were already closed. "You fly the birds, baby. Go on. Enjoy yourself." Before I could remind him that it was snowing outside, he was asleep.

Until that moment, I had never really looked at him. I had watched him, of course, every day, all the time. I had studied his movements and memorized the way he handled the birds. His expressions were so familiar to me that I anticipated half of what he did before he did it. But I had never simply looked at him.

Casey's jacket was unzipped, and his nose and fingers were bright red. I flicked on the heater and covered him with the old army blanket. He twitched but did not wake up. I fixed my coffee and squeezed back onto the far end of the bench. I had to pick up Casey's feet and rest them on my lap so we could both fit. His work boots were dirty and bits of wet leaves and mud were stuck to the treads. They pressed heavily against my thighs.

In sleep, the sharpness vanished from Casey's face. He seemed softer and more gentle. The pouches under his eyes were like small bruises, darkened by the webbings of tiny veins. His skin seemed as fragile as old paper, ready to crumble at the slightest touch. His eyelashes were short and thick and flecked with gold; his eyebrows tilted upward towards the center of his forehead, giving him a slightly puzzled look. I had never watched anyone sleep before. There was an intimacy about it that was new and vaguely exciting to me. I sat there for a long time, and gradually the anger I felt began to slip away. In its place came a new feeling, something very powerful. It was a kind of longing, or perhaps desire, to touch Casey's face.

I didn't, though. Something equally powerful held me back. Fear. Or ignorance. Or maybe I knew more than I thought I did.

After a while, I began to disentangle myself so I could go home. I couldn't fly the birds, and there was nothing left for me to do on the roof. But as soon as I shifted positions, Casey started to wake up. "Don't go," he mumbled. He raised his left hand and rubbed his knuckles hard against his forehead, as though trying to press the pain back inside. I decided to stay with him until he woke up.

15

I HAD A HARD TIME PAYING ATTENTION IN SCHOOL. MISS Haberman's fifth-grade classroom was on the second floor, in the back, and out the windows I could see stocks from half a dozen different roofs. If nobody was flying, it wasn't so bad, but if the weather was nice my eyes naturally began to wander towards the birds.

It drove Miss Haberman crazy. She tried moving my desk across the room, she kept me in late, she even sent me to the principal's office. I just couldn't seem to stop. Then one day she took more drastic measures. After school, I went up on the roof as usual, but I was worried.

When I got home, Frankie and Michael were sitting at the kitchen table slicing calluses off their hands with a razor. I slipped my key onto its nail. "What's for dinner?"

"We already ate."

"Hiya, Louie." Michael held out the razor blade. "Go ahead

and slit his throat if he won't feed you. What kind of brother are you? Give the kid some dinner."

"Cut it out, Michael. She can get her own dinner, I'm not the cook around here."

"Ma's at the store?"

Frankie nodded.

"Why does she always have to work there anyway? It's Junior's damn store."

"Hey, kiddo, take it easy." Michael reached over but I jerked away.

"Oh, shut up."

They exchanged looks and Frankie shrugged.

"What'd you have for dinner anyway?"

"We bought a pizza."

"Is there any left? I bet no."

"You're right."

I turned Michael's hand over and examined it. He had cut off the crusts that lined the inside pads of each knuckle, but the edge of his palm was a solid ridge of hardened skin.

"You get all this from working out?"

He nodded. "All the lifting. Especially deadlifts. They tear your hands up. Hey"—he grinned and wiggled his fingers at me—"how'd you like a nice rubdown with these hands?"

I made a face.

"Okay, then how about dinner? Come on, Louie, you want dinner? I'll go buy you something."

"Michael, give me a break."

"Aw, come on, man, she's your little sister. She's starving."

"She's always starving. Big deal. What are you doing home this early anyway?"

I didn't answer.

"Well, something must be wrong if you left the roof early. What happened? You have a fight with your boyfriend?"

"What do you care? And don't call him my boyfriend. Ma told you not to say that." I yanked open the refrigerator and blinked angrily at the milk bottle. "Nothing's wrong. I'm just not going to school anymore, that's all. You can tell Ma when she gets home."

I could feel both of them staring at my back.

"Louie, turn around a minute." I looked over at Frankie briefly, then buried myself back in the refrigerator. I knew what I looked like. My face was striped with dirt and my eyes were puffed and red. Pigeon fluff clung to my hair and the wrists of my sweater, and a long streak of chalky bird shit had dried down the sleeve of my jacket. My fingernails were outlined in black, and when I took my hand off the refrigerator to reach for the cheese, I left a dark grey smudge on the door.

"Louie." Frankie's tone changed. "Have you been crying? Louie, tell me the truth. Did Casey do something to you? Is that why you're crying?"

"I am not crying!" I banged open the cupboard and pulled out a cookie sheet on which I laid out four pieces of white bread. On top of each one I placed a slice of cheese, tapping it neatly into place so that it didn't overlap the bread. "For your information, Casey wasn't even up today. I was cleaning out the coops. Pigeon coops. Maybe you forgot since you don't fly birds anymore?"

"Hoo-*eey*," Michael exclaimed. "What's got into you?"

"Well, lifting weights isn't any better than flying pigeons."

"Who said it was? What's the matter with her?" he asked Frankie.

Frankie motioned for him to calm down.

113

I turned on the broiler and slammed the tray underneath.

"Louie, look, I know you're upset, but can't you even wash your hands? I'm sorry, but look at how dirty you are. Everything you touched is black. Look at it."

I looked over at the refrigerator. There was a black mark near the handle. There was one on the stove, too. I rubbed my hand even harder along the oven door till a second smudge appeared.

"Louie, stop it!"

"Well, you get dirty too, Frankie! You get dirty at the damn old Y!"

"Yeah, but we take showers afterwards. Ever heard of them?"

I bent down and peeked inside the broiler. The cheese was starting to bubble and puff up, but I liked to wait until the top turned brown. I stayed hunched over, leaning against the warmth. This was America, I said to myself. People were supposed to be free. They couldn't make me stop flying the birds. If only Casey were my father, I thought. He could take care of everything. He wouldn't let them do this. I wiped my face on my sleeve, determined not to cry anymore.

The smell of burnt toast startled me. I jerked open the broiler. A sheet of solid black cheese crusted over each slice of bread. I slid them all onto a plate and sat down at the table.

"Hey, that's all burnt," Michael exclaimed.

"No, it's not, it's exactly the way I like it." I bit into a piece and chewed very slowly. It tasted like a mouthful of charcoal.

The three of us sat there in silence. Frankie and Michael finished trimming their palms. I studied my left hand while I ate. There was a thin line of dirt under each fingernail. The fine lines and tiny crisscrossed stars that covered my knuckles were all filled in with black, as if someone had taken a single hair from a paintbrush and sketched designs all over my skin. For a moment, I forgot to be afraid.

Michael tossed his blade aside. "That's good enough. Come on you guys, let's go for ice cream." He squeezed my arm. "What do you say Louie? That'll make you feel better."

"You don't understand!" I cried, remembering. "I'm not crazy!"

"Louie, what are you talking about?"

"Frankie, they can't make me stop flying the birds, can they?"

"Can who?"

"The school? Miss Haberman?"

"Of course not. What are you talking about?"

"Oh, you don't understand!" My throat twisted into a knot and I couldn't speak. I pushed back my chair and ran down the hall into my room. I stuffed my face into the pillow, trying to muffle my sobs, and wished more than ever that I had a real door to my room. I clutched at the blanket and pounded my head against the mattress. Snot poured from my nose, clear and sticky as I wiped it across the sheets. Why couldn't everybody just leave me alone? I wasn't bothering anyone, I wasn't hurting anybody by flying the birds. All I wanted was to be left alone.

After a while, I sensed that Frankie was standing outside, trying to peer through the space between the curtain and the molding. He waited till I had calmed down, then he knocked on the wall.

"Can I come in?"

"No."

"Well, will you talk to me if I stay out here?"

"Where's Michael?"

"He's in the kitchen."

I raised my head and propped myself up on my elbows, staring straight ahead at the wall. I saw Frankie jerk his head away from the crack so I wouldn't think he was looking at me. I tugged a corner of the pillowcase loose and blew my nose on it.

"What's up, Louie? What happened?"

"Miss Haberman says I have to see the school psychologist. She's sending a note home, Frankie. She says it's not right to spend so much time with the pigeons. It's not normal. She says there's something wrong with me. There's nothing wrong with me Frankie, is there? I just want to fly the birds. She can't make me stop. It's not fair. She's got nothing to do with me, and I don't want to see a psychologist. I'm not crazy."

"Look, Louie, I can't talk to you from out here, okay?" He pushed the curtain aside and sat down on the edge of my bed. "You want me to call Ma?"

"No! Frankie, please!"

"Okay, okay." He sat with his hands on his knees and looked around. "Look, Louie, I'm not too good at explaining things, but I want you to try and understand something, okay?"

I sniffled once or twice, then turned over onto my back so I could see him. "What?"

He sighed. "A lotta guys said the same stuff about me and Michael when we started working out at the Y. 'Cause we didn't hang out as much, we still played a little football and everything, but we were always busy, always over at the Y. And they said a lotta things."

"They said you were crazy?"

"Yeah. They said a lotta worse things, too."

"Like what?"

"You know. Things."

116

"No, I don't know. What'd they say?"

"They said we were queer and stuff like that."

"Because you went to the Y?"

He shrugged. "Because nobody does what we do. They don't know what it is exactly, especially now we're doing powerlifting. It's practically a new sport, nobody really understands what it even is, so they pass a lotta remarks. And they used to say things like that when we flew birds. You can't help it, Louie, that's the way people are. If they don't understand something, they say you're crazy. There's nothing you can do about it. Just ignore them. The more you try to fight back, the uglier they get. I mean it. Don't pay no attention to Miss Haberman. Don't let her know she's getting to you, okay? I'm only trying to give you some advice."

"But Frankie, she wants me to go to the *psychologist*. Then everybody'll think I'm crazy."

"Louie, what do you care? They're not your friends if they think that. Me and Michael know you're not crazy. You're nuts, maybe, but you're not crazy!"

"Very funny! Anyway, Ma knows I'm not crazy, right?"

"Of course she does."

I sat up. "And Casey does too. He told me I was the best chaser he's ever had."

Frankie sighed. "Yeah. Casey, too."

Michael poked his head through the curtain. "Hey, I feel left out."

"Oh, all right, come in. But Frankie, what about Ma? Do you think she'll be mad at me?"

"Why should she be? You didn't *do* something to Haberman, did you?"

117

I shook my head. "She doesn't like me, Frankie. She never liked me. The pigeons only made it worse."

Michael pulled out the chair from my desk and sat down backwards, cowboy style, facing the bed. "What's going on here?"

Frankie looked at me. "Can I tell him?"

"Oh, go ahead."

Michael listened to Frankie's explanation, then burst out laughing.

"Michael, it isn't funny!"

"Of course it is, Louie. Don't you see? You go to that psychologist or whatever. You'll get a good laugh out of it. They don't do anything but ask you stupid questions. She's probably just another old maid like Haberman. It'll be a joke. You'll come back and tell us all about it. Come on, Louie, be a sport."

"But you don't understand. Maybe they can lock me up or something. That's what I'm afraid of. They'll make me stop flying. It's not fair, Michael. Maybe people say things about you, but they can't lock you up. They can't do anything to you. It's not right for them to butt into my business."

"Aw, Louie, relax! They can't lock you up. They're not gonna do anything. Look, I'll make you a promise."

Frankie rolled his eyes.

"Okay. Let's see now." Michael put his hand over his heart. "I promise that Frankie and I will never let them lock you up in the nuthouse no matter how crazy you are."

"Michael!"

"Now wait, Louie, I'm not through. Don't get all emotional. And I also promise, uh, every time they make you see this old bag, I'll buy you a malted at Frozen Fantasees. Fair enough?"

Frankie straightened up. "Michael, don't say that if you don't mean it. She's gonna hold you to it, you know."

"Hey, what kind of guy do you think I am? Of course I mean it. Whenever Louie sees the psychologist, we go for ice cream. I can see it now, she'll probably start asking to go every day!"

"Do you really mean it?"

"Louie, you're as bad as your brother. Come on. We'll go right now. Let's get this deal off the ground."

"Wait a minute, Michael, I thought we were going out. You know."

"We are. Later. We can do both. We'll settle this thing with Louie, then drop her off and go back, okay?"

"Oh, please, Frankie. I'm really hungry. Please."

He looked me up and down. "You're a mess, you know that?" He reached over and plucked a feather from my collar.

I grabbed his wrist. "Please?"

"Oh, okay. But you've got to wash up first. I'm not going out with you like that."

"Oh, Frankie, thank you!"

I flew to the bathroom and started scrubbing my face so fast the water splashed all over the floor.

"And change your jacket!" Frankie hollered.

Dripping wet, I leaned out, peeled off my jacket, and flung it at the ceiling. Dust and feathers floated through the air, and all three of us laughed.

16

M<small>Y MOTHER INSISTED ON GOING WITH ME TO THE</small> school psychologist. In spite of my embarrassment, I was secretly relieved. I had this image in my mind of an enormous figure wrapped in a white doctor's coat: an iron-jawed, steely-haired matron who would tower over me and taunt me about the birds—like Miss Haberman, only more so. In the end, however, my fears proved groundless.

For one thing, the school psychologist turned out to be a man. For another, he was young. He had a pale, boyish face and round eyeglasses that made him look like an owl. Slender and dark-haired, he wore a neatly pressed suit. He smiled. He spoke softly. He was very polite. His name was Mr. Hershkowitz, and I knew right away he wasn't going to lock me up.

Miss Haberman had told him that I was preoccupied with pigeons. He asked if I had any idea what she meant.

It wasn't pigeons in the street, I protested. That's what

everyone thought, but we hated those birds. We called them "rats," and had nothing to do with them. Our pigeons were different. They were domesticated birds called Flights that we raised and flew from the rooftops. We sent them up and tried to capture birds from the other flyers, and they tried to catch our birds. It was a real game. Lots of people played. It was like any other sport.

I stopped abruptly, fearing I had said too much. But Mr. Hershkowitz was nodding his head. "Go on," he said. "You're educating me. I've seen these flocks out here, and driving home on the B.Q.E. I see them all the time, but I never knew what it was before. I mean, I didn't know it was anything. Tell me more about it."

I looked at my mother. "Go ahead," she said. "It's okay."

And so I told him. I explained about the homing instinct and the kit-pull. I told him how we trained the pigeons and mated them up, how they courted and built their nests, how we banded the new babies in the spring. I described the feed and medicines we used; cleaning the coop; watching the eggs hatch; capturing strays. I mentioned Joey's, and flyers I had met there, and the jobs I did. I explained Casey's philosophy of catch-keep. I talked for a long time, but when I stopped I felt I'd hardly scratched the surface of the game. I hadn't realized how much I had to say. No one had ever asked.

I sat back. Mr. Hershkowitz smiled at me. "Well, I'll tell you something, Louise. You don't sound crazy to me. You sound fine. Better than fine. Okay?"

I nodded.

"Now, before I send you back, I just want to ask a few more questions, cover a few more areas. Okay?"

He asked if I had problems with my schoolwork. I said no. I

didn't like it, but I did my homework every night or I wouldn't be allowed to fly the birds.

"That sounds fair. You have any trouble with the kids, Louise? Anybody bother you?"

I shook my head.

"Any special friends?"

I said Casey was my special friend. And then I quickly added that Hector and Fingers and Joey were, too, in a way. And Michael and my brother Frankie.

Mr. Hershkowitz cleared his throat. "I'm sorry. I was talking about school. I meant any of your classmates?"

"Oh." I stalled for a minute, embarrassed. "No. Not really."

Then he asked if I had started to menstruate yet. Startled, I shook my head.

"Why are you asking about her period?" My mother seemed equally taken aback.

"Forgive me. It's just that Louise seems advanced for her age, and I wondered if it was connected to her physical development. They don't always go together, but sometimes it's a clue."

When we were through talking, Mr. Hershkowitz slipped a piece of paper into the typewriter. "Anything you'd like to ask me, Louise? Mrs. Sands?" I cringed and looked away.

"My name is Mara now," my mother corrected. Her voice was gentle. "Sands was my first husband's name. Louie's father." I could feel her eyes on me, but I busied myself collecting my books. "Mr. Sands died almost four years ago."

"I'm sorry." Mr. Hershkowitz looked up. "I didn't know. There's nothing in the notes. I'm sorry, Louise." He gestured towards a manila folder on the edge of his desk. "It's a lousy system, Mrs. Mara," he went on. "Excuse me for saying so, but it's true. Nobody should have sent your daughter here in the

first place. There's not a thing in the world wrong with her."
He spoke as if I had disappeared. "To be honest with you, I
think it's good she has something like this to do with herself.
A lot of kids here haven't got anything. That's the real problem.
Maybe Louise goes overboard, but she'll get over that."

"No I won't," I said. "Why should I?"

My mother tilted her head at me. "Mr. Hershkowitz, can I
talk to you alone for a minute?"

He nodded. "Louise, would you mind waiting outside?"

I left my books and went into the waiting room. No one else
was there, so I closed the outer door that led to the hall and
tiptoed back to the office door to listen.

"... being all men," my mother was saying.

Mr. Hershkowitz, on the far side of the room, was harder to
hear. He talked for a long time, though, and it sounded like
he was trying to convince my mother of something. She broke
in only once, to explain that she worked nights and my older
brother took care of me. I wanted to correct her: no one took
care of me anymore. I didn't need anyone. But my desire to
listen in was stronger than my wish to clarify things. Mr.
Hershkowitz said something about my father, or a father. I
didn't quite catch it. Then my mother asked him a strange
question. I could tell it was a question by the inflection at the
end of the sentence, but the only word I could make out at all
was "island" or "Ireland." My father's father was born in
Ireland, but I couldn't imagine why she would be talking about
my grandfather, whom I had never even met. Mr. Hershkowitz
said something else, but he was drowned out by the staccato
clatter of the typewriter keys while he finished typing his note.
I backed away from the door just before my mother opened it.

"Louise." Mr. Hershkowitz leaned over his desk and held out

the letter he had written. "I want you to see this. It's a memo to Miss Haberman, explaining that you are perfectly normal and do not require psychological counseling." He smiled. "Feel better?"

I nodded.

"Just try to pay a little more attention in class, okay? Save the birds for after school."

"I'll try," I mumbled.

"Good. And if you have any trouble and you *want* to see me, you know where to find me."

Ma shook his hand. "Thank you, Mr. Hershkowitz."

"Bye," I said.

I walked my mother to the front of the school. Our footsteps echoed through the empty hallways. I was afraid she would be angry about losing time from work, but before she left she bent down and kissed me.

"I love you very much, Louie. You're very special to me. I just worry about you sometimes. It's—it's hard to explain. I only want what's best for you. I hope you'll understand that one day." She hesitated, smoothing her skirt. The light skipped off her wedding band. Just then the bell rang for lunch, and everyone swarmed into the halls. I pulled away, not wanting to be fussed over in front of the other kids.

My mother walked across the concrete schoolyard and down the steps to the sidewalk. I gazed after her, immediately sorry I had not kissed her good-bye. She grew smaller and smaller as she hurried into the distance. Then she turned a corner and was gone.

17

THE FIRST BUNCH OF SQUEAKERS WAS BORN IN MARCH.
One afternoon, Casey called me over and pointed out a bird
about ten days old with an orange tumor over one eye. "You
see that baby?"

I squinted into the dark coop at one of the lower shelves. As
soon as I spotted the nest bowl, I backed away. "No, Case.
That's not fair. It's just a baby."

"It's sick, Louie. There ain't no way that pigeon's gonna
make it. You'll be doing it a favor."

"Case, I don't want to kill it. Please. I never killed a pigeon
before."

"You gotta learn." He stepped back through the opening and
knelt down in front of me. "Come here."

He tugged at my arm till I squatted on the floor in front of him.

"You done real good up here." I stared at the floor, shaking
my head. "Yes, you have. You fooled me, tell you the truth. I

didn't think you'd stick with the pigeons. You know, kids today got other interests. And anyway, you being a girl and everything, I didn't think you was gonna make it up here. But even Joey says you're good as anyone ever chased around here." He tucked a finger under my chin and tried to make me look up at him, but I just kept shaking my head back and forth.

"Hey," He placed one large hand on either side of my face, immobilizing it. "Sweetheart, listen to me." He paused. "I told you a million times, you can't get attached to these here. It's just a sport, you know what I mean?"

"But I'm not attached, Case. Honest. I just can't kill them."

"But that's part of the game, babe, and it's part of how you gotta take care of them. We ain't running no animal shelter up here. Now if a flying bird gets hurt or sick, we take care of him. But if he ain't gonna get well, you ain't helping nobody by letting him hang around. You can't spring for feed and medicine for every sick pigeon that comes along, especially now with these here babies. We got forty, fifty babies up here already this spring and another sixty, seventy coming out the next few weeks. We can't worry about one or two that's sick. You understand?"

"I know, Case, but . . ."

"No buts. You signed on as a pigeon-flyer, am I right or wrong?"

I didn't answer.

"Well, am I right or wrong?"

"Yes."

"Then you gotta learn to take the bitter with the sweet, and you might as well start now. It's all part of the game. You'll get used to it. Come on." He took my hand and led me back into the breeding coop. "Don't be afraid."

"That's not it," I insisted, but my heart was banging against my chest.

"I want you to pick up that pigeon and twist its neck." He flicked his wrist around in a motion I had seen him make many times. I had never enjoyed watching him kill the birds, but I had forced myself to, from a distance, trying to understand the motion and follow the quickness of the gesture. Deep inside, I had always known, or at least suspected, that someday he would ask me to do this. It was the hardest part of being a flyer, and I had hoped I would somehow escape it. Although I was ashamed to admit it, I had for once thought that my being a girl would work in my favor: killing was the one thing I would be excused from.

"Don't be nervous," he ordered. His voice was precise and commanding. "If you hesitate, you'll only mess it up and make everything worse. One quick twist and he won't know what hit him, but if you chicken out in the middle he'll get hurt. Okay? Just quick and steady. He's only a little squeaker so you can't miss. Go on now. Take care of your business."

I reached into the nest. The bird's mother, a yellow teaguer, backed off. The squeaker was warm against my palm and I could feel the pulsing of his whole system. He looked surprised to be snatched up, and his tiny beak opened and shut like a bellows. His thin, pink tongue curled inward in a roll. He was just a baby. He couldn't even hurt a fly.

"Stop looking at him." Casey's voice was even. "Just do it."

I stepped away. I gripped the pigeon's body with my left hand, turned my right palm against the far side of his head, then suddenly closed my eyes as my hand clutched the bird's neck. I twisted my fists in opposite directions. I was squeezing the bird so tight I could hardly feel it, and then I must have cried out because Casey opened the outer screen door and touched me on the shoulder, indicating that I should go out.

"Take it over to the trash barrel," he said. "Throw it in and don't look at it."

I obeyed. A shudder rippled through me. Only after I relaxed my stiffened hands did I experience the delayed sensation of the bird's body, like an after-image against my palms. I thought I could feel the slime of the burst tumor, but when I looked down at my hands they were completely dry.

I walked back over to the coop. Casey had already started banding the squeakers inside. Instead of joining him, I stayed where I was and rested my forehead against the chicken wire.

"Case?"

"What's the matter?"

"I think you better go over there and check if it's really dead or not. I'm not sure if I killed it all the way. I mean, maybe I just hurt it or something."

"It's dead, babe. Come on in and give me a hand."

"No, really, Case. I mean it. What if it's still alive? What if I only hurt it a little? Please, Casey, I don't want it to suffer."

"Louie." He looked over his shoulder at me. His hand completely covered the young bird he was banding, and while he paused he unconsciously stroked the bird's head with his thumb to calm him down. "He's dead."

I wiped my palms against my jeans. So I had killed a bird. That's all that went through my mind. I killed a bird. I killed a bird. I imagined tiny bones jabbing my flesh, warm blood squishing into my hands. I killed a bird. I killed a bird. I glanced over at the trash can. Maybe I should check, just to make sure. How did Casey know, after all? He hadn't killed it; I had. I started to go back. Casey wasn't watching me—he was absorbed in his work—but his voice reached me halfway across the roof.

"Louie, help me slip this band on. It's stuck."

I turned around and obeyed. The coop seemed much darker after that moment in the sun, and I had to blink away the flashes of red and purple that danced in front of my eyes.

"See this?" Casey jerked his face towards the bird's foot. "I got it caught."

I reached over. I was good at this because my fingers were small. Very gently, I twisted off the metal band, which Casey had managed to jam over only two toes. Then I gathered the three front toes together, pulled the back toe up against the leg, and slipped the ring up over everything. The freed toes immediately splayed back into their normal position and Casey put the frightened bird back into its nest. We spent the next half hour in silence, going around the coop from nest to nest. When we finished banding the babies, we fed all the birds and locked them up. Only then, after we had stopped, did I realize that my whole body ached, and my fingers felt tired and stiff.

"I think I'll drive over to Bay Ridge, pick up a few birds." Casey spoke to the sky, to the stranded tufts of clouds. I stood beside him following a stock that was rolling out over by Tito's. "Wanna come?"

I shrugged.

"Come on." He reached over and rubbed my cheek. "Take a ride with me."

He locked up and I trudged down the stairs behind him. When we got to the landing at the bottom, before we opened the door to the street, I stopped.

"Just a minute, Case. I gotta go back up. I just remembered something."

"Louie." Casey didn't even turn around. "He's dead, babe, I'm telling you. Forget about him."

18

MY SPELLING BOOK LAY OPEN ON MY DESK. THE WORDS were neatly arranged in three short columns, but I wasn't concentrating on them. Instead, I was trying to imagine what Casey's wife looked like.

He hardly ever mentioned her. I knew she hated the birds and the time Casey spent on the roof, but that was all I'd ever heard. I'm not sure when I began to wonder about her appearance. At first, I could only picture her with pale blue eyes and wavy brown hair that shone with orange and copper threads. But that was too much like Casey; that *was* Casey. I added a few pounds and substituted a bubble of mousy grey curls. The skin hung from her arms. A faded duster covered the thickness of her hips. She padded around the house in terrycloth slippers with no backs. Good, I thought. I was glad she was old and dumpy. But then I wondered why Casey would have married her in the first place. I felt a tightening in my chest: what if she was beautiful? A new image appeared. She had long, silky black hair and wore high heels and tight-fitting dresses that zipped up the back. Bracelets jangled on her arms. She smelled of exotic perfume.

The first crash of thunder caught me by surprise. The darkness had faded to a sickly yellow-green. Slashes of lightning tore through the sky. I had never seen such an explosion of rain. There had been no warning. The gutters flowed like a river. The maple tree next door lashed its heavy arms in the wind. I could just make out the figure of Mr. Laskowski rushing up the street, hunched like a squirrel as he hurried home. His umbrella was useless. The spokes had blown inside out and it soared and swooped in the wind like a crazed bat. Suddenly, I remembered the birds.

There were over a hundred babies on the roof, some only a few days old, and they were trapped in a coop riddled with holes. If they came down with pneumonia, we could lose the entire stock. At the very least, we would have to go through and inject them all with penicillin, and I knew Casey would hit the ceiling if we had to spend money on antibiotics.

I was worried about the whole stock, but the image of one particular bird pushed its way to the forefront: it was my silver dun, and she was helpless before the storm. I couldn't leave her unprotected. I had promised.

I yanked open my desk and pulled out my box of crayons. Hidden inside was a slip of paper on which Casey had long ago scrawled two phone numbers. One said "Work" beside it and the other said "Home." He had warned me not to give the numbers to anybody else, and never to call him at home unless it was an emergency. This, I decided, was an emergency.

Frankie was in his room doing homework, but his door was

open. Since the telephone was on the wall in the kitchen, I
was afraid he would hear me when I called, so I poked my head
into his room, asked him how he was, and when he said okay,
I just nodded and closed the door on my way out. He never
noticed things like that. You could walk into Frankie's room
and rearrange the furniture and he wouldn't know the difference. I was the opposite. If you so much as touched my
curtain, I would notice the change in the folds. I went to the
phone and dialed.

By the fourth ring I was ready to hang up. Then a voice I
didn't recognize snarled hello.

"Can I please speak to Casey?"

"Yeah? Who is this?"

I took a guess that it was him. "Case, it's Louie." There was
no response. For a split second I thought he didn't remember
me. "From the roof," I added.

He snorted. "I know who you are." His voice softened to
nearly recognizable tones. "What's up?"

"Case, I was worried about the birds."

"Worried?" Casey had a habit of repeating words as if they
were part of a foreign language. "What are you worried
about?"

"Case, it's pouring rain out, have you looked outside?"

There was another slight delay, and when he answered his
voice sounded husky, almost hoarse. "Raining? Nah, it ain't
raining, babe. You got the wrong station."

"Case, what are you talking about? It's pouring out there. I'm
afraid about the birds. You never fixed the roof, remember,
Case? The babies are gonna get soaked."

"Aw, get off my back. You sound just like my wife, you
know that? Ten years old and already she's sounding like my

wife. Just relax. Nothing's gonna happen." He belched into the phone. " 'Scuse me."

"Case, have you looked outside?"

"What do I want to look outside for? I'm watching television. Why don't you just turn on the television and relax? What did you call me up for, anyway?"

"Casey, please. You gotta go up and do something about the roof, the babies are gonna get wiped out. Please, Case. I'll go with you."

"You gotta be crazy. I ain't going nowhere. Forget about it. I'll go up tomorrow and fix everything up. Okay? What'd you call me up for in the first place?"

"The birds, Casey! They'll all get soaked."

"Don't worry. I gotta go, babe. See you later."

"No, wait!"

The line went dead.

I slammed the phone down and grabbed my yellow slicker from the hook. I had it on before I even went into the closet for my boots, and when I couldn't find them right away I started throwing everything out from the floor of the hall closet, including Frankie's old baseball bat and the catcher's mitt we had given him two Christmases ago, a cardboard box with Junior's old photo albums inside, and a pair of collapsible window screens.

"Hey, Louie, what's going on?" I heard Frankie's chair scrape the floor as he pushed back from his desk.

"Nothing," I said.

"Well, what's all the racket?"

"I said nothing!"

I sat down on the hall floor and yanked on the boots. Maybe Casey didn't care if the babies died, but I did. I was so mad I didn't even bother to throw the screens back into the closet. I shoved them against the wall and stomped into the kitchen for the flashlight. I didn't know what I would do when I got to the roof, but I thought I could at least see what kind of shape the birds were in and spread the tarp over the corner with the worst leaks. I patted my back pocket to feel for the keys, then, with one hand on the door, called out, "Hey, Frankie, I'm going up on the roof for a few minutes to check the birds. I'll be right back."

"Wait a minute!" He ran out of his room and grabbed my arm.

"Let go of me!"

"Well, close the door!"

"Frankie, I don't have time to argue, the babies are getting wet and I've got to go check on them."

"Not now you don't. Have you gone nuts, Louie? It's nine o'clock already."

"I know, stupid, that's the whole point. I've got to fix the coop."

"Let Casey go. He's got a car."

"He can't."

"Well, if he can't then you sure can't."

I looked away. "He's got to be somewhere. I just called him. Anyway, Frankie, I don't have time to argue. I've got to get up there."

"Not at night you don't. I'm not letting you go."

"Well, you don't have anything to say about it. You're not the boss."

"No, but when Ma's gone, I'm in charge, and if you think she'd let you go up you're really crazy. She's worried about you going up there in the daytime, let alone at night."

"She is not. Who told you that?"

"Nobody told me. I just know."

"Look, Frankie, I can't stand here arguing. The sooner you let me go, the sooner I'll be back. Now move."

He had positioned himself between me and the door and stood with his back against the lock. I reached around him and tried to grab the knob but he caught my wrist. I went to hit him but he grabbed my other arm and held me far enough away so that I was harmless. I tried kicking out, but couldn't reach him, and was slowed down by the heavy boots.

"Frankie, let me go!"

"You're not going to the roof."

"But, Frankie, I have to take care of the birds."

"Not at night, Louie. You can't go running around at night. What's the matter with you? You're acting like a fool."

"I'm not acting like a fool, idiot. *You're* acting like a fool. Now let me go."

I jerked away and tried to push him off to the side, but he yanked me by the waist and flung me several feet across the kitchen. My elbow smashed against the table. He opened his mouth as if to say something, and I could tell by the look on his face that he hadn't meant to throw me that hard.

"Get out of my way, Frankie! I'm telling Ma."

"I don't care. You're the one that's wrong."

"I'm not wrong! I'm not doing anything wrong!" Overwhelmed by frustration, I came up with the only weapon I could find. It was a word. "Asshole!" I yelled at him. I had never said that word out loud in my entire life.

Frankie looked stunned. I saw that I had hurt him. For a second I was sorry, but I would not back down.

"Asshole! Asshole! Asshole!" I shrieked at the top of my lungs. I could see the vein in Frankie's neck swell up.

"Shut up, Louie! You want every neighbor on the block to hear?"

"I don't care! Let me go! It's not fair, Frankie. I didn't do anything wrong."

"I don't care what you did. You can't run around at night."

"Well, just tell me why."

"I told you ten times already. There's a lotta creeps out there. I don't want you getting hurt."

"I won't get hurt. I just want to fix the coop or the babies'll die."

"You can't go, Louie. That's all there is to it."

I paused for a moment and fiddled with the fasteners on my raincoat as if I were getting ready to take it off. Then I twisted around and flung myself at the door. I was halfway out when Frankie grabbed me around my hips and pulled me back into the room. "Let go of me! Let go! Stop it!"

"Shut up!" he hollered. "If you don't stop this I'm locking you in. I got a test tomorrow and I'm not gonna waste the whole night listening to you bawl."

"Then let me go!"

"I can't, Louie. Now stop it, or I'll smack you so hard you won't go anywhere. You want me to call Ma home from the store?"

"No! I just want to go up for a few minutes. Please, Frankie, let me go!"

"Louie, how many times do I have to tell you? You can't go out at night. It's not safe."

"Then how come you get to do it, if it's not safe?"

"Because it's different, don't you understand?"

136

"No, I don't understand. All I understand is that it's not fair, it's not fair!"

"Louie, stop it. You're a girl, damn it."

"So what?" The tears began to rush down my cheeks.

"Girls have to be more careful."

"I am careful! I am! I am!"

"Louie, stop it! You're not going anyplace, tonight or any night. You can't go out alone at night."

"But Frankie, why do *I* have to stay inside? I'm not bothering anyone and you want to lock me up. Go lock up the guys you're talking about. It doesn't make sense."

"It doesn't matter if it makes sense. That's not the point. The point is, that's the way it is. You can sit here and cry about it all night, which is really being like a girl, or you can shut up and do something else. Just don't bother me anymore!"

"Bother *you*? You're the one that's bothering me. I didn't do a thing to you and you started screaming."

"Aw, shut up already, Louie! When you're older you'll understand."

"Why should I understand something that doesn't make any sense?"

Frankie closed his eyes. "Take your coat off. You're not going out."

I stood very still. Frankie kept one eye on me as he sidled into his room and picked up a book. "Don't try anything, Louie," he warned, settling in at the kitchen table. I stared at the seam in my yellow boots, noticing the bumps in the rubber where the sole joined the upper part. I kept my right hand in my pocket, scraping my finger along the jagged edge of my key. As soon as Frankie started scribbling, I bolted.

I got the door open and had one foot in the hallway when he

tackled me. We both went down hard, but I was ready. I slashed out at him, still holding the key, and startled myself with the sudden line of blood I etched across his face. For a fraction of a second, I don't think he knew who I was. He put his hand to his cheek and stared at me. I might have escaped in just that second, while he was in shock, but I was stunned myself and couldn't move. The skin tightened along Frankie's scalp and jaw, and his eyes glinted like hard stones. Everything became still, and in that instant of eerie calm I knew I had real reason to be afraid. Frankie raised his hand to strike me, and I did the only thing I could think of to save myself from being killed: I screamed. I screamed and howled and flailed my arms and legs. My hysteria brought Frankie back to earth. He lowered his hand. He didn't try to hit me again—all he wanted was to drag me inside before the neighbors came running. The only thing neither of us had counted on was that I had genuinely lost control, and in my rage I actually tried to fight him off, screeching and punching as he bent over me.

"Shut up! Shut up!" he ordered over and over. "Do you want the police to come?"

But it was too late. Through the living room windows, I saw the flashing red lights, and I was still beating on Frankie's back, screaming "Let go! Let go! Let me go!" when two cops arrived and pulled us apart.

"What's going on here? We got calls from down the block. What the hell's the matter with you kids?"

"He wouldn't let me go outside!" I cried.

"Shut up." Frankie's tone was calm and serious, but his orders meant nothing anymore.

"Who's in charge here?" the cop asked.

"No one," I said.

"I am," Frankie said.

"He is not!"

"Will you shut up!"

"What happened to your face, son?" The fat cop was trying to be friendly, but Frankie looked away.

"Nothing."

"Did she do that to you?"

Frankie didn't answer.

"Where's your old man?" the other cop asked.

I hated him immediately. "He's dead."

Frankie glared at me. "He means Junior and you know it."

"Well then he should say—"

The fat cop interrupted. "Do you kids wanna tell us what the problem is or do you want us to take you down to the station house?"

"Let's book 'em," the tall one said, sneering. "Looks like this one needs the fear o' god put in her."

"It's okay," Frankie said, fixing me with a sideways glance. "Everything's settled now."

"Oh, no, it isn't," I sniffed. "I'm going up on the roof and you're not going to stop me."

"Louie, will you please shut up already? Do you want them to call Ma home from the store?"

I shut up.

"It's okay, Officer."

My jaw dropped open. Frankie had never used the word "officer" in his life.

"We were just having a fight. It's okay now."

The tall cop raised his eyebrows. "You sure now? She looks like quite a handful." His laugh was ugly and sarcastic.

"Okay," the fat cop said. "Now let's straighten this out. We got more important things to do than keep you kids from killing each other."

"It's his fault," I burst out. "I just wanted to go up to the roof. I keep pigeons up there and I'm afraid it's raining into the coop."

Without batting an eye, the cop said, "You can't go out by yourself this time of night. What are you, crazy?" He smiled at Frankie. "She a nut-job, or what?" He turned to his partner. "Do you believe this? Girlie, there's a storm out there, it's dark, and you're not exactly living on Park Avenue, if you know what I mean. So give us a break, willya? We got bigger things to do than keep little girls inside after dark, okay? Would you do us a favor, huh?"

"It's none of your business what I do."

His smile faded. "Look kiddo, I don't need no lip from you. Now listen to me and let's get a few things straight. You ain't going nowhere. Your brother's the boss until your folks come home, and so help me god if I have to come back here and break things up again I'll book you both for disturbing the peace, you understand?"

The three of them loomed over me.

"I hate you all!" I shrieked. I turned to run down the hall, but I stumbled in my rubber boots and fell in a heap against the metal window screens. Without even looking, I grabbed them and hurled them at the cops and Frankie. They jumped out of the way. I ripped off my slicker, fled into my room, and flung myself across the bed, sobbing into the pillow until my throat ached and my nose was so stuffed up I couldn't breathe.

I must have cried myself to sleep, because I never heard Junior and Ma come in from the store. When I woke up, it was two-thirty. I still had my clothes on, but someone had pulled off my boots. They were standing neatly side by side in the corner.

I wrapped the blanket around me and went to sit at my desk. My eyes were so swollen they couldn't open all the way. Tears kept trickling out, but I wasn't really crying. I was too tired to cry anymore. I was too tired even to sleep. Every part of me was exhausted.

The rain had slowed to a spikey downpour. I watched it fall. That was all I could do. I was a prisoner in a cell, unjustly condemned.

Eventually, I must have put my head down on the desk and dozed off, because the next thing I knew it was morning, and the light coming in through my window awakened me.

19

B<small>Y SOME MIRACLE, WE LOST ONLY THREE BIRDS. ALL</small>
babies, dead in their nests. I had rushed up that morning to
find the entire stock huddled together in the back. I went
straight to my silver dun and quickly checked her eyes and
beak. I looked down her throat, spread her wings, and
reassured myself that she was not harmed. All the birds
were damp and chilled, though; I chased them into the sunlight
right away. Casey had been careless, but the birds had survived.

He never said a word about the storm. I kept my mouth shut,
and that weekend he finally got around to fixing the coop. I
had been watching him for ten minutes, shifting my weight
from one foot to the other while he squatted on his haunches
on the roof of the coop, laying out strips of tarpaper and
pounding in nails. I kept begging him to let me help.

"Baby, this is hard work," he said. "You can't do this."

"Yes I can! I could hold the nails or something."

Casey hooted. "I'd smash your little fingers to pieces. I told

142

you, I appreciate the offer, but I'll get this done quicker by myself. You know what you can do?"

"I'm not cleaning up the shanty."

"I wasn't gonna say that. What makes you think I was gonna say that?" He tugged his wallet from his back pocket. "Go down and buy us some sandwiches, okay?"

"Casey! You said I could help. You promised."

"This is helping. I need to eat, don't I?"

"Case!"

"All right! All right! Forget the sandwiches. Let me finish with this here and you'll help me put up the chicken wire, okay?"

I squinted at him. "Promise? I'm gonna be right over there, so call me, okay?"

"Yes, dear."

I punched him on the arm and dashed away before he could hit back.

It was the first really perfect Saturday all spring. The birds were eager to be out. They looped and rolled from one end of the street to the other. When they had cruised about a mile away, they suddenly streamed upward, hooked over on their backs, and fluttered down like a spray of confetti, sunlight shimmering off their wings. They corkscrewed high above the neighboring factories, bound together by nothing but instinct. There was no leader, and not even the best flyers like Casey or Fingers could predict what their movements would be. But somehow the birds knew. Some invisible signal was passed along and the birds responded. Day after day they soared and tumbled, streaked and turned, flying by magic as one bird. And when they were done, if they were good flying birds, even if separated they would land only on their home roof. From the day they were born till the day they died, they would never touch the street. I leaned on the parapet at the back of the roof and stared out at the murky blue-brown of the East River. A few boats trailed up and down, cutting calm, deliberate paths through the water. I wondered where they were going, and what they did, and who sailed on them.

At my feet was a pile of tarpaper scraps. We called them "scalers," and sometimes Casey tossed them in the air to spook the pigeons and make them fly in different directions. If one hit near the center of the stock, the piegons would scatter like spilled corn. I sat down and sorted the scalers into piles, according to size. After waiting what I thought was a reasonable amount of time, I strolled back to the coop.

"Ready for me yet?"

"Almost. Tell me something. Did you see who's got his birds up today?"

I looked around. Besides ours, there were only a couple of little bundles out. I had hardly noticed. "I see Mooney's, and I guess that's Gus's birds over towards Union Avenue, right?"

"Yeah. And who else do you see?"

Our stock was dipping over the gas tanks near Maspeth. The sky was a creamy blue, the same color as the plates in a diner. There was no glare to mask the birds from me, but no matter where I looked I couldn't spot any other stocks.

"Come on." There was an edge to Casey's voice. "It's a beautiful day out, perfect flying weather. Tell me what kind of competition we got out there."

"Casey, give me a minute. I'm still looking."

He stopped pounding. "Don't waste your time."

"What do you mean?"

"I mean, that's the point. These goddamn mutts don't have

any birds up! You understand what I'm saying, Louie? It's Saturday morning, clear as a bell, nice gusty winds, and these beggars are home snoring! What kind of pigeon-flyers are they! It's a beautiful day! They should all take their birds and go open up a farm, 'cause that's what they are, a bunch of fucking farmers. I'm sorry, that's the only word for them. They don't play for the sport no more, Louie. It makes me sick. They're all saving their birds. They toss them up just enough for exercise, then breed whatever they hear someone wants. They're so worried about losing, they don't play no more. It's bad enough we lost hundreds of flyers over here when they started putting up the projects, and the same thing across the bridge, on the Lower East Side. At one time every other building over there had a coop on it. I'm not kidding, Louie, there were tons of flyers. Then they knocked down all the tenements and put up projects, and all the flyers disappeared. Some of them started over, but a lotta guys, the old-timers, they gave it up. But what gets me is, what's left over here, they don't even fly no more. Not like they used to. They keep up like this, the goddamn game's gonna die out. I mean it. There ain't gonna be nothing left." He banged a few nails into place, then stopped to survey his work. "That ought to do it, don't you think?"

"Let me see." I scrambled up next to him and looked over the fresh black patches. "Looks good to me, Case. You did a nice job."

He scooped up the leftover nails and poured them into a rusty soup can. Then he hopped off the coop and I followed.

"It's a shame you weren't around before, Louie. There used to be so much action out this way, you'da loved it. You'd be busy from morning till night. I mean really busy. Guys used to come up the crack of dawn, we'd plan chuck-ups and everything just to get things moving."

"What's a chuck-up?"

"When the guys get together, they each agree to bring like fifty or a hundred birds to one spot, then let them out all at once so they'd get mixed up like crazy. We used to let them out over in McCarren Park sometimes. It was wild. You could get a thousand birds up there, all tangled up trying to get home, and sometimes we'd lose a ton of birds, everybody would, but it was fun, you know? It was exciting. Nowadays these geeps worry so much about every single bird, it's a pain in the ass, Louie, I'm telling you. The sport ain't what it used to be, that's for sure. There used to be some great old flyers around, guys who really stirred up the action. We used to have some good times here." He laughed. "You know who used to be a great flyer?"

I shook my head.

"Angelo."

"Angelo! Come on Casey! Are you kidding?"

"Unh-unh. He's been over there on Grand Street for forty years. Forty years on that same roof. And he used to be wild. He *flew* his birds. I first met him when he and this guy Fish were in the middle of this big war. They had a real feud going on over on the Southside."

"Fish! What kind of a name is Fish?"

"That's just what they called him. He ran a fish store. He and Angelo had a war going ever since they was kids practically. You know what they say down at the pet store, about 'Enemies on the roof, friends in the street?' Well, that's horse shit. These guys hated each other everywhere. They practically killed each other over the birds. They did all kinds of things."

"Like what?"

"Oh, like one winter Fish caught one of Angelo's birds and he tore one of its legs off and sent it back."

"Casey! That's terrible. Did the bird die?"

"Unh-unh. That little sucker lived another five or six years. Angelo kept him like a pet, he took care of him. He didn't fly with the stock no more, but he was okay. He took care of that bird like he was a baby. Angelo was all right. I mean, that's what gets me sometimes, these guys didn't used to be this way, little crybaby mutts afraid of losing a bird or two. They used to be sports."

"Even Fish?"

"Yeah. Him too. He was okay. I didn't like him, though. He was a ugly bastard. I mean, whoever heard of ripping up a bird like that? I don't like that stuff."

"Joey said there was a guy named Dominic who used to bite the heads off pigeons and eat them."

"What are you talking about?"

"That's what he told me! And he said during the Depression, guys made soup out of their birds. He said they had to, just to feed their families."

"Yeah, they made soup all right, but I never heard that about Dominic. I just know these two guys had a feud going on as long as anybody knew them. Till Fish took a heart attack and died."

"What did Angelo do about the bird?"

"He didn't do nothing. He took care of him, disinfected the stump I guess. Nobody knows why it lived, it was just one of those things. But the next time Angelo caught one of Fish's birds, he took care of him, all right."

"What did he do?"

"He kept him, of course—I'll say that much for them, they always played catch-keep back then. So, Angelo waited till the next day, when he saw that Fish was up on his roof, and he hollered out, 'Hey, I'm sending your bird back! Merry Christmas!' And he tossed up the bird, and attached to its leg was one of those little red Christmas tree ornaments, you know those shiny little balls? Only Angelo had filled it with gunpowder, like from a cherry bomb, and lit a fuse to it. That bird was halfway home when it just went boom! Exploded all over the place right in front of Fish's eyes. Everybody in the Southside saw it, that was all they talked about for months. Fish couldn't walk into a pet shop anywhere in Brooklyn that someone wouldn't ask him what he fed his birds that made them blow up in midair. Angelo definitely came out of that on top. The two of them didn't even speak to each other after that. Not a word. They wouldn't even be in the same pet store together. Angelo told me—after Fish was dead—he told me that Fish had come up to him in the street one time and said, 'Enough's enough. When are we gonna be friends again?' And you know what Angelo told him? Angelo looks him in the eye, real calm, and says, 'Don't worry. I'm just waiting. As soon as my bird's leg grows back, we'll be friends.' "

"Does Angelo still have that bird?"

"No, not no more. He died a couple of years ago. Now Angelo's a geep like everyone else. He got old, Louie. He stopped looking for the action up here." Casey dragged over the roll of chicken wire. He shook the coil loose, then flipped it on its side and rolled it out against the roof. He grinned. "Don't ever let me catch you getting old, you hear me?"

"Uh-huh."

"You promise?"

148

"Promise. You're not old, are you, Case?"

He looked around. "Where are my clippers?" I picked them up and held them out to him. "I'll be thirty-nine in May. That's getting up there."

"May what?"

"May twenty-seventh. Why?"

"I just wondered. Case?"

"What?"

"Weren't there ever any flyers that you liked?"

"Sure. I just told you, Angelo used to be okay. Gus is a nice old man. Joey's all right. He's not the smartest guy, but he's got a good heart."

"But I mean someone who was a friend. Someone you really liked."

He snapped the clippers open and shut a few times. "Yeah. There was a guy I grew up with, Richie. We used to be pretty close."

"Which one is he?"

"Nah, this is going back before your time. He used to fly over on Metropolitan Avenue. He was a real sport. Chased his birds up every chance he got. He didn't care who else was up there or how many of his pigeons they caught. He loved to fly the birds. That's the only thing he got out of it. Pleasure. He liked to watch them fly. He could lose a hundred pigeons in one day, he'd still come down to the shop with a smile on his face. 'Hey! I had a good time,' he'd say. He was a real sweetheart, nicest guy in the world."

"Where's he fly now?"

"He don't."

"How come?"

" 'Cause he's dead, that's how come. Here take this. Mark me

149

off forty-eight inches." He flipped me the tape measure. "You don't fly pigeons when you're dead."

Casey started cutting the wire while I leaned on it to hold it in place. When the piece came loose, he carried it over to the coop and we each took an end and stretched it out over the old section.

"That looks about right, don't you think?"

I nodded. "What happened to him?"

"To Richie? He—I don't know. It's a long story."

Casey clipped the old wire and started ripping it off. The rusted tacks flew out in all directions.

"He was too good, if you know what I mean. He didn't think things through like he should have. If someone asked him a favor, bing, bang, bong! he'd do you the favor. He never asked no questions. That's what he was like. He trusted everybody. That's no good, Louie. You gotta take care of yourself, and Richie didn't do that. And if you're too good to people sometimes, they take advantage of you. It ain't right, but that's the way people are."

"But what happened to him?"

I had picked up the box of wire tacks and poured some into my hand, and from these I selected one at a time to hand Casey.

He tried to grasp the nail I was holding out to him, pinched between my thumb and forefinger, but his fingers were too thick, and the nail fell to the roof without a sound. Casey shook his head at me. "You can't do it like that. Just hold them open in your hand and let me take them, okay?"

I opened my palm and waited. Casey worked quietly for a while, but after a few minutes, without breaking his rhythm, he began to talk. "I don't know why I'm telling you this, Louie.

I don't talk about this stuff to nobody." I made a point of studying the nails. "See, Richie was in love with this chick for years, girl named Barbara—'Babsie' they called her—who was a real bitch, if you'll excuse my language. I mean from the gutter. You know what I'm saying? I mean, the nicest girls from the neighborhood woulda loved to go out with Richie, but he had to love this piece of junk. She fu— She went to bed with anything that moved. A real sicko. And Richie was in love with her. I mean the guy loved her, he made excuses for her up and down the street, he even asked her to marry him. He figured all she needed was to settle down and be married and everything would be okay. And she married him. She was no fool. Richie was her meal ticket. He was a real sucker. It was like he was bewitched, I'm not kidding you. He just wouldn't see what she was."

"Why did he love her if she was like that?"

"Why? *Why* did he love her? You can't say why. It's just something that happens. Jesus Christ! Who knows why anybody loves anybody?"

"Okay, okay, I'm sorry I asked. Go on."

"Anyway, after they got married, nothing changed. I mean, I told Richie that, everybody told him that, but he just wouldn't listen."

"What do you mean?"

"I mean, she still ran around, you know what I'm saying? She was unfaithful, Louie. That ain't the half of it. And Richie used to pretend everything was okay. But meanwhile, while he was out working, she used to bring her boyfriend home. To the house. In front of the whole neighborhood. It's like she wanted to get caught or something. It was just a matter of time. So finally that's what happened. Richie walked in on them, just like in the movies."

"What were they doing?"

Casey gave me a puzzled look. "Louie, do you understand what I'm talking about?"

My cheeks burned. "Of course I understand! I just meant—oh, never mind. Just go on, okay?"

"I woulda killed them both right there on the spot, but not Richie. He walks out without saying a word and gets drunk for three days, sleeps in his car. He went crazy-like, Louie. He never was a really big drinker or anything, he was just quiet, you know, a real sweetheart, and then after this he started falling apart. I mean, it wasn't anything new, she'd been running around since the day they'd met, but he just kinda pretended, I guess. I don't know what else you'd call it. How could he not know? But then when he found her with this guy, he got crazy."

"Did he get a divorce?"

Casey shook his head. He stopped pounding nails for a minute. "Nah, he didn't get no divorce. You know what he did? He went out and bought her a six-hundred-dollar fox jacket, can you believe what I'm saying? He bought her a coat! And he told me they was working it out. He said she promised him it was all over. I was like his best friend, Louie, we stood together for years growing up over there, and I never saw anything so pathetic in my whole life. He went broke buying her things, like that was supposed to make her happy. And all the time she went right on seeing this other shit. And Richie went right on buying her things. He even bought her a gold watch. I'm telling you, it made me sick. I told him not to do it, but he wouldn't listen to nobody. You know what he told me? That sucker told me, 'She's coming around, Casey. She's coming around.' The hell she was. I swear to god I wanted to go out and kill her myself."

"Casey!"

"Aw, Louie, you don't understand."

"Well, why didn't he just leave?"

" 'Cause like I told you, she opened up his nose. You understand me? She opened up his nose so wide you coulda built a goddamn highway through there."

"I would never love someone who was like that. I think it's terrible."

"Yeah? What do you know about love anyway, Louie? You're ten fucking years old."

"Well, I know something!"

Casey started hammering again and we stood in front of the coop, a few inches apart, shouting above the noise.

"You know something about love? Yeah? What do you know? You ever been in love?"

"Maybe!" I clenched my fists, having forgotten the nails in my left hand. Their sudden pricking against my flesh stung so sharply that I scattered them across the roof

"You don't know, Louie, so don't talk about things you don't know!"

"I do too know!"

"Yeah? Who you been in love with? Hector? That's your idea of love, some skinny kid who's got his brains up his ass? You should talk."

"I am not in love with Hector and you know it!"

"Well, who's the lucky guy, then? Who taught you so much about love you can pass judgment on everybody else?"

I glared at Casey, and he glared back. His eyes were exactly

153

as blue as the cloudless background against which he stood, and for an instant I had the distinct impression that I was seeing straight through him to the sky. We had faced off, like enemies, ready to fight.

I could have answered him then. For once, I had the words I needed—actually, it was only one word—but I didn't say anything at all.

"That's what I thought. You're too young, Louie. You don't even know what I'm talking about anyway, do you?"

"I do too!"

"Yeah?" Casey turned back to the coop. "I don't even know why I started talking about all this again in the first place. How'd we get on this subject?"

I had to think for a minute. "Because I asked you if there was ever a pigeon-flyer that you really liked."

"Oh, yeah." Casey set the hammer down on the steps and laced his fingers through the wire, staring into the darkness of the empty coop. "You know what he finally did, Louie? He went up to his roof one afternoon—this guy who had never done one rotten thing in his whole life—he went up to his coop, he's got maybe a hundred, hundred-fifty pigeons up there— and he killed every single one of them with his own hands, wrung their necks one after the other, every single bird he owned. Then he went downstairs to his apartment, and he took his wife's gun—his *wife's* gun, you hear what I'm saying? —'cause Richie himself never owned a gun, he didn't like them. I'm telling you, this guy wouldn't even go fishing, that's the kind of guy he was, he couldn't stand to see nothing killed— and he went into the bathroom and blew his fucking brains out. Stupid fucking bastard!" Casey was gripping the wire so tight that it cut into his hands.

"Casey! Be careful." I took a step toward him. "Case, are you okay?"

He nodded.

"Case?" I lowered my voice. "Why are you mad at *Richie*? You sound like you're mad at *him*."

"Damn right I'm mad at him! He was my friend, Louie. I loved that guy. He shoulda killed that bitch of a wife and her boyfriend, that's who shoulda died, not Richie."

"I still don't understand why he didn't just leave her."

"Aw, fuck you, Louie!"

My head snapped up. Casey had never said that to me before. Never. Not even when he'd been drinking. I lowered myself to the nearest step. Casey looked at me and started to say something, but I turned away from him. "Well, *I* would have. How can you love somebody like that?"

"I told you, don't go talking about things you don't know nothing about. He loved that goddamn broad. She made him crazy, you understand me? He did things for her you wouldn't believe, he was insane."

"Well, I thought if you loved somebody you were supposed to be good to them."

"He *was*. That's what I been telling you. He was *too* good. You don't even listen to what I'm saying."

"But I mean *her*, Casey. She didn't love Richie, did she?"

"Of course not. She didn't love nobody but herself."

"Well, that's what I'm saying. If she didn't love him, why did he stay with her?"

"Because *he* loved *her*. That's enough. That's love, Louie. You'll do things like that when you love somebody. You'll do things you wouldn't do for anybody else. Just wait till you're older. It makes you crazy. You can't understand this stuff now. You're too young."

"Well, why'd he have to go kill all the pigeons, too?"

Casey stared into the distance, following the spray of black pinpricks that was our stock. "That was his way of letting her know he understood what was going on. You gotta realize something. See, this mutt she was involved with, he was pretty hot shit over there. He was mixed up in a lotta things. And she thought Richie believed her, that it was finished. She thought he was that stupid. That's what kills me. Richie acted like everything really was okay, he never gave no sign like he knew what was happening, even with me, and I was his best friend. We used to go out together and everything, he even played dumb with me. But the truth is, he knew all along she was still seeing this guy. And this geep was also a pigeon-flyer." Casey shook his head before I even got the words out. "Unh-unh. You don't even want to know. You don't want to know scum like that exists. See, Richie knew that if he killed himself, he never had no chaser up there with him, he didn't have no relatives that flew pigeons, he knew what would happen to those birds."

"I don't get it."

"Think about it. His wife would give them to her boyfriend. He was a flyer. He would of took all of Richie's stock. That's why he killed them, so that Ni—so that this creep couldn't get his hands on them."

"Nicky! Nicky who hangs out at the pet store? I thought Nicky was married!"

"Who said anything about Nicky? I didn't say no names."

"But you started to say—"

"I didn't say no names, Louie."

"But Casey—"

"Louie, that's enough. I didn't say no names. I shouldna told you nothing to begin with."

"That's not fair! You always say that when I ask something."

"I always say that? Is that a fact? I swear to god, Louie, I talk to you more than anybody else. It's unbelievable. I tell you things I ain't never told nobody. How can you say that to me? But some things you can't say to nobody, you don't understand that. This here what I told you is strictly private, I don't want you repeating it to nobody. Especially not Hector, not anybody down there, you understand me?"

"Casey, you know I never tell anybody what you say."

"Well, keep it that way."

I bent over and started hunting for the nails I had dropped.

"Let them alone." Casey took my place on the steps. "We'll sweep them up later. Come sit over here with me. Come here." He patted his knees. I straightened up and walked over, then hesitated. "Come on, sit down here a minute. It's okay." He reached over and helped me onto his lap, and I leaned against him, my head nestling underneath his chin. His beard tickled my scalp and made the skin tingle on the back of my neck.

"Listen, Louie, I'm sorry I said that to you before."

"Casey, I promise I won't tell anybody! I swear!" I tried to look up at him, but he pressed my head back against his chest. He was wearing a flannel shirt, and it felt soft against my cheek.

"No, baby, that's not what I meant. I meant, I didn't mean to say 'fuck you.' I shouldna said that to you. I'm sorry."

"Oh. That's okay." Neither one of us moved. "Case, can I ask you something? Can a man still have a girlfriend after he gets married?"

"Louie, let's not talk about them no more. Please."

"I'm not. Honest. I'm just asking. I mean people in general. Can you do both?"

"Baby, why don't you ask your momma about this stuff? You're too young to think about these things. Really. This ain't something for you to worry about."

"I'm not worried. I just wondered."

"Well, ask your momma, okay? I think that's who you should talk to about this kind of thing."

"I already know what she'll say. I'm asking *you*. You said I could ask you anything up here. You always said not to be afraid."

"Yeah. I was talking about the birds, though. You can ask me anything you want to know about the pigeons. That's what I meant."

"Please, Case. Just answer this one question and I promise I'll stop bothering you, okay? Please?"

He leaned back and readjusted me on his lap. "Yeah. I guess so. Sometimes."

I turned my face farther into his chest. "That's what I thought." Casey tightened his arms around me. My shoulders were jammed together, and my nose was pressed so hard against his ribs that I could hardly breathe. But I didn't say anything, even though it hurt, because I didn't want him to let go.

20

Joey's feed supplier drove in from South Jersey every Wednesday morning. My first job that day was always to open one of the fifty-pound sacks and re-bag it into five- and one-pound packages. A lot of kids in the neighborhood—some only six or seven years old—flew pigeons, and they could neither carry nor afford the large sacks. Sometimes they didn't even have the money for a pound. They'd plunk down a few pennies on the counter, and Joey would pour them out a scooperful of corn. He never let anybody's pigeons starve.

I was weighing feed and humming to myself when I glanced up to find Hector standing in the middle of the shop. Before I could say hello, he swatted his hand at me to keep still. Joey and Fingers went on playing gin.

"What happened to him?" Hector's voice was very low.

Joey picked up a card from the pile and inserted it into his hand. He discarded carefully before answering. "He's gone."

159

"Who?" I asked.

"Gone where, Joe? What happened? His roof's empty. The birds is all gone, the coop's dismantled, everything."

"Who are you talking about?"

"Hector, take it easy," Joey said. "Come over here so we can talk."

Hector didn't move. "I want to know where he went. He was expecting me. He wouldn't just leave town like that. He woulda told me if he was leaving."

"Who?"

Fingers sighed and flipped his cards over. Joey scooped them up and patted the deck back into shape before setting it aside.

"Louie." Fingers reached into his pocket and jingled some change.

I shook my head.

"Come on. Be a good kid and get us coffee."

"Unh-unh. I gotta finish this today. Sorry." I turned back and poured another scooper of corn onto the hanging scale. Fingers put the money back in his pocket.

"Hector, sit down," Joey said. "Listen to me. Please. Sit down."

Hector ran his hand through his hair, then crossed over and pulled the chair up right next to Joey.

"Don't bullshit me, man."

Joey stared down at the table. "Listen to what I'm gonna tell you and don't ask questions. Ray is gone—for good—you understand what I'm saying? He ain't coming back. Don't go up to his roof and don't talk to nobody. Don't try to make no deals. I'm telling you, Hector, things are gonna get very ugly here for a while and you don't want no part of it. Keep your mouth shut and stay out of it. They ain't fooling around."

"But why, man? Why him? What's happening?"

"There's a lotta things you don't know, Hector."

"I know what was going on! I ain't stupid!"

Fingers slammed his fist down on the table and the cards skittered to the floor. "You wiseass kid! You don't know *shit* about what was going on over there, and if you keep shooting off your goddamn mouth about it, thinking you're so big, some of them other assholes are just stupid enough to believe you. For once in your life, do something smart, you hear me? You're not gonna get two chances. The less you say, the less you're around for a couple of weeks, the better off you'll be. Don't go over there, and don't trust nobody. You're nothing to them. Anything you got, keep to yourself. Don't try selling it now, I'm telling you."

Hector looked away and began drumming his fingers on the table. "Well, Ray told me a few things. He trusted me okay."

Fingers looked at him for a long time. "You know, you're dumber than I thought," he said quietly. "Go on then. Go spread it around. You knew what was going on. He told you things."

Hector looked over his shoulder at me. "What are you staring at, stupid?"

I bent over the bin and plunged my hands into the corn.

"You know, Louie, you get on my nerves sometimes, you really do! You don't even know how to bag the goddamn feed!" He started towards me, then changed his mind. He walked quickly out of the shop and slammed the door.

I taped shut each of the small paper sacks and lined them up on the shelf. Then I went over to the table. "Who was Hector talking about? That guy Ray that Casey knows?"

Joey looked at Fingers before he nodded.

"What happened to him?"

"He went away."

"Where'd he go? Florida?"

"Yeah," Joey said.

"No," Fingers answered at the same time.

I looked from one to the other. Finally Fingers spoke. "He's dead."

I had never seen Fingers like this. I scratched at a clump of gummy dirt on the table till it came off, then I brushed it onto the floor. "How come Hector's so upset? He wasn't friends with him, was he?"

"No, not really."

"We're through playing cards, right?" Without waiting for an answer, Joey grabbed his rag and returned to his familiar post behind the counter.

"Well, then, why's he so upset?"

"Huh?"

"Why is Hector so upset? Why'd he yell at me for?"

"He don't mean nothing. He just—I don't know, Louie. Sometimes a person thinks he knows a lot more than he really does. Sometimes somebody can even tell you certain things, like, in order to make you think you know a lot, when really they're just telling you what they want you to know in the first place. That make sense?"

I shrugged.

"Not really, huh?"

"No, not really."

"What I'm trying to say is, a lotta people don't always do the right thing. Sometimes they can sort of set someone up, make them think they know a lot about something, but really all they know is just what you want them to know. I can't explain it.

Hector's a good kid, see, but he's Puerto Rican. Those guys he works for aren't gonna let him in on much, they're just using him, really, but he don't see that. He did a little something for Ray, made himself some money, now he thinks he knows everything, and if he goes around shooting off his mouth, he's gonna be in serious trouble. What he should do right now, the next couple of months, is to stay quiet and mind his own business till all this blows over."

"All what blows over?"

"There's some guys around here that's having a disagreement over a few things, like a war I guess you might call it, with some guys from East New York."

"Did Hector do something wrong?"

"No, not exactly. He's a good kid, Louie. That's why he should stay out of all this. But he had some stuff he was supposed to hold for Ray, and now they gotta sort the thing out, like who should get it and so on."

"Is it something illegal?"

"Louie, this is Hector's business, okay? Don't ask me no more questions."

"Does Casey know about it?"

"Look, Louie, there's a lot of things Casey does, I look the other way, believe me. It ain't none of my business. But Hector's just a kid, what is he, sixteen, seventeen? And Casey did the wrong thing here, that's all I'm gonna say."

"But what did Casey do?" I begged. "I thought he did Hector a favor. That's what Hector told me. He introduced him to Ray so he could get a job."

"That's enough. They got the kid involved in a lot of things I don't think he should be handling. But Casey don't stop and think. That's his problem. He just don't think."

163

"But Hector wanted this job. He told me. He asked Casey to help him. He said he didn't want to end up mopping offices like his old man."

"Louie, don't misunderstand me. I ain't blaming nobody. I'm just worried Hector's gonna do something stupid on his own, and none of us can stop him. He won't listen to nobody."

"Maybe Casey could talk to him."

Fingers shook his head.

Joey stopped wiping off the counter. "Wait a minute," he said. "Why not? It's worth a try."

Fingers shrugged. "I don't think so. Casey's into a lotta bucks with them. Ray or no Ray, he's still gotta pay them back. He might see a way to get something out of it, who knows?"

"But he's not gonna risk—hey, come on. You know him better than that."

Fingers kicked at the scattered cards. "I don't know nothin' anymore, Joe. Louie, look at me." I thought he was going to ask me a question, but he didn't. He just studied my face for what seemed like a long time, as if I might somehow tip the balance of his thoughts. Finally he looked away. "I guess it's worth a try," he said.

21

EVERY TIME I LOOKED AT HECTOR I GOT THE
giggles. He was wedged underneath the shelf in the shanty,
squatting like an oversized hen so he wouldn't be seen, and I
was trying in vain to push his bony shoulders even farther
down. He moaned and made faces at me until I was laughing
so hard I could barely get the candles lit.

"Do you think Casey'll be surprised?" I whispered. I ducked
under and jabbed at Hector's elbow. "Do you? Tell me the
truth. Honest."

"Shorty, if you ask me that question one more time he'll be
surprised to find you minus a head!"

I fell over in hysterics. I thought that was the funniest thing
anyone had ever said.

"Louie, shut up! They'll be here any minute. Joey already
whistled."

"Okay." I bit my tongue. "I told Joey to go real slow on the stairs." I couldn't help it; I burst out laughing all over again. Hector looked completely disgusted with me.

I clapped both hands over my mouth and waited.

Finally, their voices drifted in from the landing and we heard their footsteps cross the roof. I clutched Hector's arm. The door to the shanty was flung open and everything happened all at once: I yelled "Surprise!" much louder than I meant to; Casey's jaw dropped and his face was briefly flooded with an orange glow; Hector banged his head trying to stand up; and the draft from the open door blew out all the candles.

"Oh, wait! Don't look!" I cried. "Hector, help me! Please!" Hector was rubbing his head. I shoved the matches at him.

"What is this?" Casey peered around the shanty as if something might be lurking in the semidarkness.

"Nothing! I mean, happy birthday! Hurry, Hector! Casey, please, just come all the way in and shut the door already! And don't look!"

"What the hell's going on here?" Casey was trying not to smile.

Joey helped Hector, and they finally got the candles relit. They were now of distinctly different heights, but it was clear to me that this was the best we could do. I touched Casey's hand. "Happy birthday," I said. "I'm sorry. It was supposed to be a surprise."

Casey stared at the cake. He kept shaking his head back and forth. After a very long time, he just said, "Shit." Admiration, surprise, and tenderness were all mingled in that one syllable. My month of planning, saving, dreaming, had been worth it, just to hear the way he said that word.

Casey touched the cake lightly with one finger, as if he didn't quite believe it was real. "That's beautiful! No kidding, I never saw nothing like that. Where'd you get that, Louie? You didn't make it, did you?"

"No! Mr. Montanero made it, at La Scala's."

"Oooh, they're good! Joey, do you believe this? Will you look at this cake?"

"It's beautiful," Joey said.

I thought it was more than beautiful. It was perfect. With translucent jelly icing, Mr. Montanero had painted a pigeon coop. Dozens of tiny birds—each one a delicate V—were flying out the door and scattering across the sky. Around the border of the cake, instead of rosettes, were thirty-nine larger V's made of yellow icing, into which I had inserted thirty-nine candles, and one to grow on in the middle. Across the top, in red letters, it said, "Happy Birthday, Casey."

"You planned all this by yourself, Louie? You got the cake and everything?"

I nodded.

"Just for me?"

I nodded again.

"No kidding. Nobody ever gave me a surprise party before, never. Never in my whole life, I swear to god."

Hector tapped him on the arm. "Blow them out, man, they're melting all over everything."

"Yeah. Okay." Casey kept looking at the cake and moving his head from side to side. At last he leaned over and inhaled.

"Make a wish first!" I cried. "You've got to make a wish!"

He scratched his beard. "What am I supposed to wish for?"

"Anything. Whatever you want. And don't tell anybody."

He stared at the candles for a moment, then blew. Because they were arranged along the borders of the cake, he had to make a full circle to catch them all, and there were a few candles still flickering when he finished. He snuffed them out with a couple of short breaths, and we all applauded.

Casey looked around. "Hiya, Hector," he said, as if he hadn't really noticed him before. "How's it going?"

Hector held out his hand. "Not too bad. Happy birthday."

"Yeah." Casey nodded. He looked over at me and laughed. "You're terrific, you know that?" He kissed the top of my head.

"Let's cut the cake! Hiya, dolly." Joey patted my cheek. "You did a nice job here, you really did."

"Thanks."

Casey grabbed a knife from the top shelf. "I don't know how to do this," he said to me. "Maybe you should do it, I don't want to mess it up."

"You won't mess it up. It's your birthday, you're supposed to cut it. For luck."

He eyed the cake, then began sawing at it until he had severed a section about three inches wide. He split that into halves. "Get me a plate, willya, sweetheart? Jeez, you've practically opened up a store in here."

I handed him a plate and he gave the first piece to Joey. "Here you go. Happy birthday."

"It ain't my birthday," Joey laughed.

"You want a fork?" I asked as the cake was already halfway to his mouth.

"Nah, I don't need that."

"Hector?"

He shook his head.

I sighed and put the forks away. I should have known better. Casey cut two more slices, for us, and we all ate in silence. The cake was delicious, and for once I ate slowly, letting the tiny crystals of sugary icing melt on my tongue. It took me awhile to notice that the silence was growing awkward. I blurted out the first thing that came to mind. "I'm sorry I don't have any ice cream."

Joey nodded and said, "This is fine, dolly."

Then Casey's face lit up. "We got something better than ice cream. 'Scuse me." He brushed past us and returned a second later with two six-packs of beer he had stashed in the old refrigerator behind the shanty.

"This is more like it." He offered the beers around. Joey and Hector seemed grateful for something cold to drink. I would have liked something myself—it was unusually warm, even for late May; I was actually beginning to sweat—but there was no soda left. Casey had forgotten to buy it when he'd brought up the beer.

"Let's go sit outside," he suggested. "It's too crowded in here." He set his cake down on the counter. I must have made a face because he called over his shoulder, "I'll finish that later." But I knew he was just saying that. Hector followed him over to the steps of the coop and sat down. Joey hung back for a minute.

"Everything okay?"

I didn't look up from my plate.

"That cake sure was good."

"Casey didn't seem to think so."

"Aw, sure he did. You know he don't like sweets too much anyway."

"Not when he's drinking, you mean. I should have given him beer for his birthday, that's all he really likes."

"Come on, don't say that. He loved the cake. I never seen

him so surprised. You heard him, nobody ever surprised him like that before."

I set my plate down next to Casey's and sucked the icing off my fingers. Joey put his arm around my shoulders. "I know he's really glad you did this. He just don't show it right maybe, you know what I mean? Come on, it's a little cooler outside. Come sit over here, okay?"

"I'll be there in a minute. I want to put this stuff away first." I flicked on the light and pretended to clean up. There wasn't really anything to do, so I rearranged the napkins and forks and threw out Hector's empty plate.

I joined the three of them on the steps. Casey motioned for me to sit beside him. Joey passed Hector a cigarette, which he smoked with all four fingers over the top. He was showing off for Casey. He even accepted a second beer. Behind us, inside the coop, the pigeons went on bubbling and cooing.

This was my favorite time on the roof, with the sun low over the city and the sky becoming gradually muted and streaked with a hazy rose-colored glow. Lights were just beginning to flash on: streetlights, headlights, neon signs. Office windows in Manhattan turned into tiny gold squares, and silvery airplanes became indistinguishable from the surrounding skies. The streets once again grew quiet, like early in the morning. When Joey began to talk, his voice was so soft it almost seemed like part of the night.

"I remember once I got a surprise. It wasn't my birthday, but I was around twelve, thirteen years old. I had been involved with the birds a couple of years already. My uncle had birds, my father's younger brother, he was about twenty-five." Joey chuckled. "I thought he was *old,* can you believe it? 'Cause I was just a kid then, I guess. I didn't have much to do with him 'cause I was chasing for these real old-timers, two fruit peddlers, Ira the Jew and Willy. Anyway, he had a lot of birds over on Broadway, and one day he just disappeared. Took off one morning and never came back. Vincent, his name was. Vinnie. We never knew for sure what happened to him. My father thought he had joined the Marines at first so nobody worried too much. He figured we'd hear something sooner or later. In the meantime, they gave me the keys to the roof to take care of the birds. My father gave me money for feed and stuff, thinking Vinnie would get in touch, but he never came back. Nobody ever heard a word. So I just inherited the whole stock, my first real stock of flying birds. Eventually I got a job over at the sugar factory, sweeping up and cleaning, to earn money for the pigeons. You remember that place?"

"You really worked there?" Casey exclaimed. "I heard stories about that place that'd make you swear off sugar for the rest of your life."

"Nah." Joey glanced at me. "It wasn't that bad."

Casey finished his beer and tossed it aside, not even aiming for the trash barrel. "You remember Diamond John, that big Polack lived over on Newel Street?"

"Piggy's cousin? Sure, I remember him."

"Well, he was a packer over there, and he told me one time they didn't have no toilets where they worked. They were supposed to wait until their break because you had to go on the outside about a half a block away to the main offices to take a leak. So he told me that all the guys that worked there used to go to the back where they had this huge mound of sugar, about fifteen foot high, and they'd piss right there into the sugar. Can you believe that?"

"Uggghhh!" I said. "That's disgusting."

Joey looked away. "Nah. I don't think they really did that, that's just the kind of stories they tell."

"How could you eat that stuff?" said Hector.

"You eat sugar all the time!" I cried. "You eat piss and don't even know it!"

"Louie, what kind of talk is that?" Joey turned to Casey as if I weren't there. "See what you started? Look at the way she talks. That ain't no good, Casey, I'm telling you, that's what they been talking about."

"What who's been talking about?" I demanded.

"I don't tell her to talk like that."

I pulled at Joey's sleeve. "What who's been talking about?"

"Well, don't talk like that in front of her."

"Louie, talk like a lady." Casey's order was perfunctory.

"I don't want to be a lady." I turned to Joey. "He can talk however he wants. If he can say it in front of Hector, he can say it to me, right, Case? Casey can say anything in front of me he wants."

Casey looked away. "Joey's right. Maybe I forget. I get carried away."

"Well, thanks a lot," I snapped. "I thought I was supposed to be your chaser. Hector's not even anything up here and now you'll tell him things but you won't tell me."

"Take it easy. What are you getting so excited for? This ain't got nothing to do with pigeons. What's the matter with you? We're talking about other things, which you don't say when there's girls around."

"But I'm not a girl, Casey, I'm just me!"

Casey raised his eyebrows and looked me up and down. "You look like a girl to me," he said. Something in his voice made me blush.

"You know what I mean!"

"Now, dolly, don't get upset," Joey broke in. "Nobody meant no harm. We're trying to be nice to you. You gotta learn not to let guys talk like that in front of you in the first place."

"But I don't mind. Why should I care?"

"Well, of course you care. Guys don't like a girl to curse and talk nasty, and they don't respect you if you let them talk like that."

"But everybody talks that way, Joey. I hate it when they shut up because I walk into the shop or something. You know how they do. And then they get mad at me. Well, I never asked them to stop. They can talk however they damn please for all I care. How do you think it feels to be treated different all the time?"

"Okay, that's enough." Casey put his hand on my shoulder. I shook him off.

He quickly popped open another beer and handed one to Hector. Joey refused his and stood up. "Well, I gotta go," he said. "I gotta get back to the shop. Butchie's watching it for me and I don't like to leave him alone too long." He tilted his head toward the shanty. "Thanks for the cake, dolly. It was a nice party."

I got up, still sulking, and walked him to the doorway.

"Bye." He patted my head. "You coming in tomorrow?"

I nodded. "For a little while."

"Okay. See you then."

He had already disappeared when I remembered my manners. "Thanks for coming!" I called into the darkness.

Hector hung around for a long time, talking to Casey. At one point, they seemed to be arguing, but then they calmed down. I began to think Hector was never going to leave. He even

drank a third beer, and Casey broke into the other six-pack
for himself. Casey was sitting on the top step leaning against the
coop, his legs spread wide apart. Hector sat in the same
position, trying to look like Casey. I couldn't stand it anymore. I
inched towards them, pretending to be watching the street, but
the closer I got, the lower their voices became.

The breeze had died down and the stickiness of the night was
more apparent. No one noticed when I took out one of the
beers. I sat down two steps below Casey, my back in the space
between his knees, and picked up the church key lying by his
foot.

"I honestly don't know," Casey sighed. "End of summer
maybe. Maybe never."

"It can't be never, man. I need the bucks. I think he's okay. I
think he's one of Ray's guys."

"We'll see, Hector. Just be cool, okay? Don't do nothing now.
Remember what I told you. Now let's talk about something
else."

"You don't have to," I piped up. "I know all about Hector's
job. I know all about Ray and everything."

Before they could raise an eyebrow, I pried the cap off the
beer and took a sip. My mouth puckered at the bitter, rusty
taste, and I had to force myself to swallow.

"What the hell are you doing? Give me that." Casey grabbed
for the beer but I pulled my hand away.

"Louie, you ain't drinking no beer! What's the matter with
you? You don't even like that shit."

"Well, I'm thirsty!"

"So go get a drink of water. You ain't drinking no beer."

"Oh no? Just watch me." I tipped the bottle back and took
another tiny sip, but before I could get it down, Casey

174

snatched the bottle out of my hands and hurled it against the wall.

"I told you not to drink that!"

"Well, Hector got to drink it!"

"You ain't Hector! What's the matter with you?"

"How come he can have it and I can't?"

" 'Cause he's older, for one thing. And it ain't ladylike."

"Well, fuck ladylike!" I screamed. "Hector gets to do everything! It's not right. I invited him up here in the first place."

"Well, then be a little nicer to your guests, why don't you, and stop being so ugly. I don't want no more fighting up here."

"I'm not fighting. I just want to know why he gets to do everything and I can't!"

"Because he's old enough to drink beer and you're not. Okay? Now will you just settle down and relax for a change? Jesus Christ."

"Well, I get thirsty, too, you know! Don't I count?"

"Yeah. Go get yourself a drink. You forget where the hose is?"

I backed away a few steps. "Anyway, the party's over," I announced. "It's time to go home." I folded my arms across my chest and turned my back to them both.

"Okay. Well, so long, man." Hector stood up and they shook hands.

"You think about what I told you," Casey said.

"I will." Hector tapped me on the shoulder. "See you, Shorty. Thanks for the cake."

I wheeled around. I was going to say something nasty, but

175

Hector was holding out his hand to me. He had never done that before.

We shook hands and said good night.

Casey sat back down. I trudged over to the shanty and tossed out his half-eaten piece of cake.

"Baby, shut that light, willya? You're drawing a million flies over there. And turn on the radio. Let's have a little music. This here's supposed to be a party." Casey's voice was thick and husky. I glanced at him before flicking off the light. He was slumped against the coop and his eyes were closed. This time I planted myself on the same step, a little to his left. I leaned up against the coop like he did and stretched my legs.

For a while we listened to the radio without speaking. I plucked at my shirt, which was stuck to little pockets of sweat along my chest, and gazed at the sky. The stars were coming out, and thin, transparent clouds hung overhead. I leaned forward and sighed.

"What's the matter now?" Casey didn't open his eyes.

"Nothing. I'm going to get a drink of water."

I stood up and tucked in my shirt. The hose was coiled at the far end of the roof, and as soon as I lifted it up my hands got streaked with the rusty grime from the nozzle. I couldn't wipe them on my clothes, as I would have done under normal circumstances, because in honor of Casey's birthday I had put on clean khaki shorts and a blue blouse. I had even washed my sneakers. I walked over to the stairwell and grabbed a rag. When I stepped back onto the roof, Casey had stood up and was unbuttoning his shirt. I looked away. I had seen Michael half-naked a hundred times and it never embarrassed me, but the sight of Casey's bare chest, smooth and already slightly tanned, made me feel shy. His nipples were pale, more pink than brown, and unlike the rest of his muscular, work-hardened body, his stomach was soft and slightly rounded. As he strode over to the hose, his shirt flapping open, the skin prickled along the back of my neck. He turned on the spigot and took a drink. I hung back in the doorway until he waved at me to come over. "This'll cool you off. Come on."

I took a step forward.

"Here, come on. Drink it like this. I won't get you wet." He cupped one large hand over the hose and filled it with water, then offered it to me. I guided his fingers to my mouth and took a few small sips. His hand was bigger than my whole face, and in contrast to his blunt, thick fingers, mine looked like skinny little pigeon toes.

"You want more?"

I was enjoying the roughness of his hand in mine, but I shook my head no. He wiggled the tip of the hose in my direction. "Wanna really cool off?" His eyes twinkled.

"Noooo!" I backed away and blocked my face with my arms.

"Okay, okay, take it easy." He stripped off his shirt and placed his thumb over the nozzle. He aimed the spray over his chest and shoulders and the back of his neck. Then, using his shirt for a towel, he dried himself off and tossed it aside.

"Come here, sweetheart." He opened his arms and grinned at me. "Let's dance."

I looked down, my face flaming. "Casey, I can't dance," I mumbled.

"Neither can I," he laughed. "We're perfect partners." I didn't move. "Come on," he urged. "It's my birthday. Dance with me." He tugged my hand, and the next instant my cheek was pressed into the softness of his belly. I was not prepared for the warmth of his skin. I was pinned so tightly against him

177

that every part of my body seemed to be touching his, and the slight pressure from his fingers seared into my back like the blaze of a branding iron. For an instant my left hand hovered gingerly above his belt, then I rested it against the small of his back. I had never touched anyone's nakedness before. I couldn't think of anything to say. I tried concentrating on the music: Bobby Darin was singing "Mack the Knife." I knew the song—they played it all the time—but I had never been able to understand the words.

Casey guided me across the roof, needing only the slightest shifting of his knee against the inside of my thigh to direct me. We glided back and forth across the roof. Then, without warning, we stopped. He slid his other hand around my back and curved his body ever so slightly until I felt something move, a slow stirring against my middle, as if some living thing had slipped or fallen in between us. I straightened my back.

"Don't get nervous." Casey's voice was both command and reassurance. The pressure of his arms kept me close, and in a flash of intuition I realized what was happening. Michael and Frankie in the living room, mimicking Mr. Cunningham. Fragments of that half-understood conversation returned and pieced themselves together at last: Casey was having an erection. This was what they had been talking about. It was his penis that I felt, rising against my body, making its cautious, uncontrollable exploration even through the layers of our clothing. I had never thought about it moving all by itself like that, a simple surge of flesh. I had never really thought about it at all. Yet there it was, happening right between us. Casey's penis had stiffened into this mysterious soft-hard bulge, warm and thick and firm, held in place by the nearness of our bodies. I was suddenly afraid to move; I was also afraid not to. As we

stood there, barely rocking, something indefinable altered all
around us. The air seemed to quiver and grow still.

It took me a minute to figure out what was wrong. "Case?"
My voice was muffled against his belly. My lips brushed his
skin as I spoke. "Casey, the song is over."

"Don't worry about it," he said gruffly.

I looked up at him. His eyes were closed, and he gripped me
in the darkness, swaying very gently to a rhythm I could no
longer hear. The deejay's voice rose and fell as softly as a
shadow, and Casey bent his knees and arched his pelvis into
the soft center of my body. The movement could hardly have
been considered a real thrust, but I was ten years old,
straddling a narrow fence between wonder and fear. I cried out.

Casey let go of me at once. A coolness rushed in where his
body had been. "My god, Louie." He hit the side of his head,
like a swimmer clearing water from his ears. "Jesus Christ. Go
get your things, I'm taking you home."

"But, Case, I thought you wanted to dance with me. I
thought—"

"We done enough dancing. Let's go. Come on."

Casey didn't look at me the whole way home. I wanted to
apologize, but I didn't know what for. I had liked dancing
with him. I didn't want him to let go. It was just—the rest of it.
I wasn't ready for that. But how could I explain? What could
I say? I didn't even understand it myself.

By the time we reached my house, I was miserable. "I'm so
sorry, Casey," I burst out. "Whatever I did up there, I'm
really, really sorry. Please don't be mad at me. Please."

Casey lowered his head until his forehead rested against the
steering wheel. "You didn't do nothing, Louie, you hear me?

It's my fault. I'm the one that should be sorry." He sounded very tired. I reached over and touched his knee.

"I just wanted you to have a happy birthday."

"Yeah." He patted my hand and placed it back on the seat. "I did, baby. Thanks. Go on in now. Everything's okay. Just forget about it, okay? I'll see you tomorrow."

I said good night. Inside, I took my time getting ready for bed. I washed. I brushed my teeth. I studied my face in the mirror. Casey had danced with me. I wouldn't forget anything. Ever. I undressed in the darkness of my room. A feather was snagged in my shoelace and I tugged it loose. It was a primary tip, pure white, in perfect condition. I held it to the window, to catch the glow from the streetlight, and then I saw something that made me step back: Casey was still parked in front of the house, his head resting on the steering wheel. He hadn't moved an inch. I watched him for a long time, waiting for something to happen, but nothing did. After a while, he simply lifted up his head and drove off.

I sat down at my desk and opened the top drawer. In the back I kept a large brown envelope filled with photographs. Most were of Poppy, but some were of Frankie and me when we were very small. I undid the metal fasteners and slipped the feather inside. It was the only place I could think of where it would be safe.

22

THE HOT SPELL LASTED UNTIL THE END OF JUNE.
At its worst, it was almost unbearable. I couldn't stay in the sun
for more than an hour at a stretch, and sometimes Casey
didn't come up at all. The birds grew gaunt and listless. Even a
short fly exhausted them. Their beaks hung open and their
necks throbbed. One morning I saw one of Angelo's birds stop
in mid-flight and plunge straight down into the street. Casey
said it was a heart attack.

In that kind of weather, I hated cleaning the pigeon coops.
They were poorly ventilated, and inside the dead air hung
motionless for days. Dirt and dust soaked up all the moisture.
When you inhaled, you breathed in something dry and
powdery, more like flour than oxygen. But it was my job, and
with school out for the summer I really had no excuse.

Casey was asleep in the shanty when I began, and I was
trying to finish before he woke up. Arms aching, grimy,

drenched in sweat, I moved mechanically down the rows of nest boxes. I had to go through every single one with a paint scraper and loosen the accumulated mess. On the floor I would do the same thing using a snow shovel. When all the crust was broken up, it got swept into the trash. Then I would wash the whole place down with the hose, spraying especially hard over the screened sections, where debris collected around the tiny hexagons of chicken wire. I was still scraping boxes when my ears began to ring. I stopped to rest. For a while the ringing continued; then it changed to a light tap-tapping, a distant, unfamiliar sound. It took me a minute to realize it wasn't coming from inside my head. Someone was coming up the stairs. I peered through the screen, thinking it must be Hector, and was astonished to see a woman standing in the doorway. She was wearing a peach-colored sundress and white high heels. A mass of curly blond hair framed her face. She was plump, almost heavy, but curved rather than thick. She had very big breasts.

I tossed the paint scraper aside and she jumped.

"What do you want?" I said, stepping out from the screen.

"Oh. I'm— Hi. I'm looking for Casey." Her chest was still heaving from the climb. "Is he up here?"

"Who are you?"

"I'm Casey's— I'm, uh, I'm Arlene. I'm a friend of Casey." She smiled. Her lipstick was bright pink. It matched her nails.

"Why are you wearing those shoes up here?"

She blushed and took a step backward. "I'm sorry. Isn't it okay?" With her feet together, the flare of her hips was even more pronounced. Her body seemed inflated, swollen beyond normal size. In comparison, I felt flat and two-dimensional.

"I just meant because of the shit. And sometimes you have to move fast."

"But I'm just looking for Casey. I saw his car downstairs. Isn't he here?"

"Casey doesn't like visitors."

"But he told me to come up. He said he'd be here all day."

"He told you to come up?"

She nodded.

"Wait a minute." I took my time crossing to the shanty. "Casey, there's a girl here for you." I shook him by the shoulder, harder than I had to.

"Ow! What's the matter?" He jerked up.

"Nothing, Case. Relax. There's some girl here. You want me to get rid of her?"

He looked around. "Hey! Come on in," he called.

"Hi, Casey." She waved at him.

"Hiya, sweetheart. Come on in. Don't be scared. I ain't gonna bite you."

She leaned over him and they kissed each other on the lips. "Hmmmm," Casey purred. "Maybe I *will* bite you!" He kissed her again.

I banged open the storage bin and filled the coffee can with corn. I did it automatically; the birds had already been fed.

"Casey, you're not mad about last night are you?" She sat down next to him.

"Nah, don't worry about it."

"It's just that my mother hasn't been well, and when she called, I just felt like I had to go over there. I got scared."

"It's okay. These things happen. Of course, they don't usually happen just at that particular moment!"

She turned bright red. "Oh, Casey, I'm so sorry! I really am."

He touched her hand. "Don't worry about it. It's okay."

Arlene glanced at me. "I could make it up to you, you know."

"Yeah? Is that a fact?" Casey's voice was low and teasing. He cleared his throat. "Louie, how about running down for some coffee? This here's Arlene."

"I can't. I'm cleaning the coops." After a pause, I added, "She should've brought it up herself if she wanted it." I slammed into the main coop and attacked the far wall, scraping box after box without pause. All the soreness was gone from my arms. Droppings crumbled to dust and sailed through the air. I had no idea how long I worked. I screeched the snow shovel across the floor, swept everything up, and hauled the trash can out to the stairwell. On my way back I glimpsed only one face in the shanty and felt relieved. I should have known Casey would send her away. She didn't belong on the roof.

Instead of unwinding the hose, I tossed out a handful of corn and the birds fluttered down for the unexpected treat. I flipped the net over my silver dun and carried her inside. She was very warm; her heart thumped rapidly against my hand. I sat down in the empty coop, ruffling her neck feathers and crooning into her ear. But the image in the shanty returned. Something about it disturbed me: the angle of Casey's head, the slackness of his jaw. Suddenly I knew he was not alone.

I jumped up. The motion made me dizzy. When I stepped into the sunlight, still clutching the dun, the distant rooftops shimmered in the heat. I headed for the shanty. My eyes were fastened on the window, which revealed more and more with every step. Casey's head was thrown back and his eyes were closed. His arms were tensed at his side, his hands gripped the bench. I took one more step and stopped dead in my tracks. A tangle of blond hair was thrust deep between his thighs, pink nails were splayed against his jeans. I absorbed all this in a fraction of a second, not understanding what I saw. I was aware only of some powerful, violent act for which I had no name. That, and the burning whiteness of Casey's flesh, the terrifying flash of skin where his fly had opened and his jeans had bunched up below the crotch. I turned and fled back to the coop.

I must have blacked out for a moment. When I came to, I was lying on my stomach in the darkness. Something was stuck under me, pressing against my ribs. I pulled myself to my knees. Sweat was pouring from my forehead, and I lifted up my shirt to wipe my face. Then I saw the dun. Her neck was twisted backward on itself, her beak broken at the nostril, her eye open, startled and gleaming in the half-light of the coop. She rested with an awful stillness at my side.

Without warning, a spasm racked my body. I doubled over and threw up. Then I collapsed against the wall.

I stared at the dun for a long time. She had been my bird. The only thing on the whole roof that had ever really belonged to me. I knew what I had to do, but it took me a minute to get my strength back. I braced myself and thrust her lifeless body under my shirt. Holding her gently in place, I ran out of the coop and down the stairs. Casey never noticed my departure.

23

THE HOUSE WAS EMPTY. I WENT STRAIGHT TO MY mother's room and, without hesitating, turned the key in her cedar chest. Inside were her best sheets and linens, things she hardly ever touched. They were saturated with the warm, pungent smell of the wood. I pulled out a dish towel embroidered with purple flowers and wrapped it around the dun. Then I carried her back to my room and carefully laid her into an old shoe box.

I could have buried her in the backyard. That's what I wanted to do. The only problem was, Mr. Laskowski stayed outside all day, fussing over his tomatoes, and he would have seen. I didn't want anybody to see. They would ask questions and expect me to explain, and that was something I could never do.

Instead, I carried the shoe box over to McCarren Park. My plan was to find a quiet spot under a tree and dig it up with a

stick. But the ground was harder than I thought. I got nowhere.
In desperation I tried gouging out a hole with my foot,
kicking over and over with my heel. A nun walked up and
asked if anything was wrong. Behind her, people were staring
at me. I said no and hurried away.

Why hadn't I noticed? There were people everywhere,
lounging on blankets, playing softball, walking their dogs.
Drunken old men were sprawled out on the benches, babies
screamed in the grass. I scoured every inch of the park, from
the rest house to the bocci court, but it was a summer day: there
was not a single private place. I crossed back over to Driggs
Avenue and headed home. On the corner was one of the city's
metal garbage cans. I stopped and closed my eyes. "I love
you," I whispered. Then I kissed the shoebox and stuffed it in
the trash.

Afterwards I was in a state bordering on panic. My appetite
disappeared. I did nothing but lie in bed and listen to the
radio all day. At night I did the same thing. I had trouble
falling asleep. Often I woke up sweating long before daylight.

When Ma and Frankie asked about the roof, I made excuses.
I didn't feel well, I said. They could see that for themselves. It
was the heat. I needed a few days' rest. They exchanged looks,
but didn't press me.

Everyone was preoccupied. Frankie spent all his time with
Michael. Junior's sister-in-law filled in at the store, and Junior
and Ma took the car and disappeared for hours at a time. They
ducked in and out all day, making phone calls, shuffling
through papers, talking about the bank this and the bank that.
Ma stayed home at night and made more phone calls. They all
existed in another world. I noticed but attached no significance
to what they did. It didn't concern me.

187

One morning I dragged myself into the bahtroom and discovered a dark stain in my underpants. I started to cry out, but caught myself just in time. I took a closer look. It was the blood of my first period. Sometime in the night it had arrived. I hadn't felt a thing. When I told Ma, later in the day, she said it was a sign that I was growing up, that wonderful things were about to happen to me. But she was wrong, and I knew it. It was just the opposite. Everything was over for me now.

24

I TRIED NOT TO THINK ABOUT CASEY. IF THAT WAS
what he wanted—a girl who wore high heels on the roof—that
was fine with me. Let her be his chaser. I didn't care. I was
never going back.

I was never going anywhere. That's how I began to feel after
a while. I never went out. Some days I hardly even left my
room. One afternoon I decided to write a letter to Paulette.
Except for the Christmas cards, we didn't really keep in touch,
but I missed her and wondered if she missed me too, sometimes.
I thought maybe she could come for a visit. I started the letter,
'Hi! How are you?' Then I drew a blank. So much had
happened since I'd seen her last. How could I explain
everything? I tried over and over, but I couldn't find the right
place to begin. Finally, with a pile of wadded up pages on my
desk, I gave up.

Two weeks went by. Then one evening Casey showed up at

the house. At first, when Ma told me, I didn't believe her. I rolled over and faced the wall.

"Louie, he's in the kitchen. He wants to talk to you."

I sat up. "He's here? In the house?"

Ma opened my dresser and handed me a T-shirt. "You want to change, baby? That's a little rumpled."

"Did he say what about?"

"He'll tell you. He wants to tell you something. You want to see him, don't you?"

I pulled on the clean shirt. Ma raked her fingers through my hair, combing out the tangles. "Louie, I'm—"

"What's the matter?"

"No, nothing. I put out some root beer. You can offer him some."

"Is Frankie home?"

"No. No one's here. Frankie went someplace with Junior. They won't be home till late. I'll stay in my room."

I waited until I heard her door close, then I went out.

Casey was still standing near the entrance. He smiled at me. "So, how you been sweetheart?"

"I'm okay."

"Just okay? That don't sound too good. That's how you been, just okay?"

I nodded. It was hard for me to look him in the eye. "Come in. You want some root beer?" I got out the ice and went over to the sink. "Go ahead and sit down if you want." I filled the first glass too full and had to wipe up the counter. I spilled some out, then carried them both very carefully over to the table. Something didn't seem quite right. I felt unsettled, and it took me a minute to realize why: Casey was sitting in my place.

"So," he said again. "How you been?"

"Okay," I said. I sat down next to him. "How are you?"

"I'm good. Everything's okay. What's new with you, sweetheart? I haven't seen you for a while."

"Nothing."

"Nothing? Well, I didn't see you for a few days, I thought I'd stop by."

"A few days? You haven't seen me for over two weeks!"

"Is it that long? No kidding. I had no idea it was that long." He drank half his root beer in one gulp. "So, you been okay?"

"I'm fine. Stop asking me that."

He looked away. "You got a nice place here. It's comfortable. I like that."

"Casey, why did you come here?"

"Why did I come here? I just told you. I wanted to see you. Louie, I gotta talk to you about something."

I held my breath. Now he would explain. He would apologize. Everything would be all right, and nothing would ever interfere with us again.

"I know," I said. "About what happened on the roof, right?"

"Louie, look, you don't have to say anything about that. Don't worry about it. Everybody gets sick sometimes. It was a hot day. I ain't mad at you."

He wasn't mad *at me*? "Casey, what are you talking about?"

"Louie, forget it. I hosed down the coop. That's the end of it. It ain't worth worrying about."

"Oh, Casey." I almost laughed. Was it possible that Casey didn't even *know*? Did he really think I'd stayed away because I was embarrassed, because I'd thrown up in the coop? I stuck my finger in my glass and twirled the ice. Or did he think *I* wanted to pretend?

191

"Louie, listen to me." Casey tapped the edge of the table. "That's not what I came up here for. I don't understand how everything got so messed up in the first place. I make a lotta mistakes, Louie, but I swear to you I never meant for anything like this to happen. Everything's gotten crazy lately. You wouldn't believe the kinda pressures I got sometimes. Sometimes I think I'm going nuts, sweetheart. I really do." He stopped abruptly and tried to laugh. "Aw, don't mind me, baby. I'm talking crazy now. Don't pay no attention. You feeling okay, Louie? I mean, for real? You're not sick or nothing?"

"No, Casey. I'm okay."

He pushed his glass aside. "Louie, Hector's dead. He was shot this morning in East New York. I didn't send him. I swear to god. I told him not to go."

No, I thought. I had been away two weeks. I hadn't seen Hector, that was all. He wasn't dead. Just because I was away. What Casey said didn't make any sense.

"Louie, I'm sorry. I wanted you to hear it from me."

I shook my head. Hector was alive. He was standing on the roof, by his run-down coop, feeding his birds. Or maybe he was at Joey's, arguing with Nicky or sweeping out the back coop. Or he was home in bed, for all I knew, wherever home was, fast asleep. Casey had misunderstood, like he misunderstood everything.

"Louie, did you hear me? Hector was shot. He's dead."

"Will you please stop saying that!"

"Louie, listen to me! It's true. I'm sorry, baby. But you gotta understand something. There's guys down at the shop gonna say I sent him over there. I'm telling you that never happened. I want you to know that. I had nothing to do with it. I told him not to go, but I couldn't stop him. I don't care what anybody tells you, that's the truth." Casey got very quiet.

"What happened to him?" I asked finally.

"Louie, what difference does it make? It's ugly, baby. You don't want to know this stuff."

"Tell me what happened."

"Hector got involved with these guys, small-time stuff, making deliveries and things."

"What kind of things? Drugs?"

Casey hesitated. "Sort of. Yeah."

"For that guy Ray?"

"Yeah."

"That's the guy who came on the roof, isn't it? The one who got killed?"

"Louie, I just introduced him, that's all. Ray needed someone and Hector was begging me to introduce him over there. I never dreamed he'd go and do something like this."

"But what did Hector do?"

"He tried to work out something on his own. This guy called and set him up. Hector thought he was okay, he used to be one of Ray's guys, so he trusted him. But everybody told him not to go. It was too risky right now, they're still sorting out everything. But he went anyway, Louie. He thought it was his big chance. I'm sorry, baby. I really am."

I stared at the table. There were patterns in the Formica, white swirled through white. I couldn't believe I would never see Hector again.

"Louie, are you all right?"

"I'm fine."

"It's okay to cry or something. Hector was a good kid. I know you liked him a lot and I know he—"

"Oh, shut up!"

Casey sat back, as if I had hit him. He hadn't understood one single thing. He had no idea what the last few weeks had been like. What I had been feeling, what I felt for Hector, these were feelings that didn't show. It was a kind of sadness on the inside, where you couldn't see. On the surface, I was numb.

We sat in silence. Casey finished his root beer and stood up. "Look, Louie, tomorrow, if you want to, your momma said you could go to the wake with me. I could pick you up after work."

I nodded.

"I'll come by about four, four-thirty, okay?"

I walked Casey to the door. "Couldn't they just scare him or something?" I asked. "Why did they have to kill him?"

"I don't know, babe. That's the way they do things over there." He turned to look at me. "Tomorrow, after we're through over there, what do you say we go up to the roof for a little while, okay? You'll come back with me, what do you say?"

Casey hadn't apologized, he hadn't understood, and everything wasn't all right again. But I still said yes.

25

MY MOTHER SAT ON THE EDGE OF HER BED AND FINISHED buttoning my good dress. It was navy blue and had a white lace collar. I didn't even remember putting it on.

"Louie. You have to change your shoes now, too, baby. You want me to get them?"

I looked at my feet. "These are clean."

"No, Louie, I'm sorry. You can't wear sneakers to the wake."

"Okay."

"It's disrespectful. You wouldn't want Hector's parents to feel insulted, would you?"

"It's okay, Ma. I'll wear the others."

"Oh."

While she was out of the room, I wandered over to her dresser. Her collection of perfumes was arranged on a china tray. The bottles were all different shapes and sizes, and their amber tones were shot through with gold from the afternoon sun. Casey would be by for me any minute. I picked up each bottle in turn, pulled out its glass stopper, and sniffed.

My mother came back and set the shoes down, but I didn't turn around. I went on fiddling with the perfumes. I rearranged them, shifting the larger ones to the back, edging the little ones forward. I didn't say a word. I shuffled the bottles back and forth. I sighed. I lined up the round ones on one side and the square ones on the other.

Finally, my mother said, "Louie, would you like a drop of perfume?"

I shrugged.

"It's all right. A drop won't hurt you. Which one do you like?"

I poked the smallest bottle to one side.

"This one? Okay, turn around."

I looked up into my mother's face. She tapped the stopper on the rim and quickly dabbed it behind my ears. She barely touched me.

"Now put your shoes on. Hurry. I want to talk to you."

I followed her out to the sofa in the living room.

"Here." She handed me a mass card. "Give this to Hector's mother. She'll be in the front row of the chapel. Or his father. It doesn't matter."

I nodded.

"Louie, I want you to know something. It's up to you. I mean—the coffin will be open, baby, that's how it's done. I'm sure Casey will go up to pay his respects, but you don't have to. It's—strange, sometimes. People look different. It's not like sleeping, I don't care what everybody says. Sometimes it's better not to look, and just remember them the way they were, alive. You understand?"

I walked over to the window to watch for Casey's car. "Ma?"

"Yes, baby?"

"Did I look at Poppy?"

"No." She started to get up, then changed her mind. "You were too little then."

In the car with Casey, I thought about what she'd said. I already knew how I wanted to remember Hector: the way he looked Thanksgiving morning, at Joey's, showing off his Homer in the box. I didn't really want to see him dead. But Hector was my friend. If that was how you paid your respects, then I would pay mine like everybody else. I would glance in just long enough to say good-bye, then I would look away. I didn't want Casey or anybody else thinking I was too little anymore.

The chapel was dark and cool. I looked all over, but none of the flyers were there. Casey went straight to Hector's parents. They seemed to recognize him and said something to each other in Spanish. Casey said, "I'm sorry. I'm really sorry." I didn't know what to say. I held out the mass card. "Hector was my friend," I whispered. I don't know if they understood.

The casket rested on a kind of altar that was covered in velvet. I held Casey's hand and fixed my eyes on the floor as we walked over. My heart was racing. I didn't look up until the last possible minute, and then I saw immediately that all my resolutions had been in vain. The coffin was closed tight.

Afterwards, Casey said he felt hungry and asked if I'd mind stopping off somewhere. I said it was okay with me, and he drove over to the Triple Decker on Metropolitan.

We slid into a booth. I had never been to a restaurant with him before; it was almost like being on a date. We ate pie and

197

coffee without saying a word. I didn't care. Casey and I were friends again. We didn't have to talk.

On the way out, I asked him why Hector's coffin had been closed. He said he didn't know and to stop asking so many questions.

Things more or less returned to normal. I was back on the roof and at the pet shop. Nobody mentioned Hector, though, and nobody asked me where I'd been. One afternoon I was up flying the birds by myself when Bennie set off a bunch of firecrackers. The stock scattered in a million directions. I got a kind of chill, and all of a sudden I understood what had really happened, why Hector's coffin had been closed. Nobody had to tell me. I just knew. Hector had been shot in the face.

26

"I'M NOT GOING!"

Frankie, Junior, and Ma stared down at the kitchen table. We had been sitting there a long time, getting nowhere.

"I'm sorry. I'm not going. You all can move to Islip if you want, but I'm not leaving."

"Louie, how many times do I have to go through this? You're not making it any easier. The main reason we're moving is for you and Frankie. Why do you think Junior and I have been working two jobs all year? Junior hasn't slept more than five hours a night for months. We want to get you kids out of here, to someplace clean and safe. I especially want to get you into a better school."

"But I don't care about school anyway. What's the difference, here or there? I won't like it out there any better."

"I think you will, Louie. At least give it a chance."

"Aw, Louie's gonna love it once she gets there." Junior's voice boomed with a phony cheerfulness. "Louie, we got a nice big house out on the Island, and you've got your own room—with a door."

"I don't want a door out on the Island. I want a door right here, on my real room!"

"Look, Louie, you complained about that room all year. Now we're getting you out of it and you don't wanna go. That don't make sense. And try thinking about someone else for a change. After we move, your mother won't have to work night and day anymore. She can do more things with you, take you places, go shopping with you."

"I hate shopping and you know it!"

"Louie." Ma sounded tired, but I didn't care. I steeled myself. "Look, baby, let's not argue anymore. I knew this would be hard for you, but I honestly thought you'd be a little more willing to give it a try before you made up your mind."

"Well, I'm not!"

"Well, you don't really have a choice."

Ma had spoken, but I glared at Junior. What did he care if we left the neighborhood? He had nothing to lose. He could have a grocery store anywhere. But what about me? If we moved to the Island, how was I going to fly the birds? There were no Flights out there. They were all Homer guys or show types. How would I get back to North Eighth Street every day?

My mother rubbed her forehead. "Louie, it's a final decision. I know you're upset about it right now, but this move is really for your benefit. I think that once we're out there you'll like it a lot better than you think. We have a yard and everything. We could even get a dog."

"Who wants a dumb dog?" I sneered.

"Well, I just thought you might want a pet. I know how you love the pigeons."

"Ma, the pigeons aren't pets! You don't understand. I don't want a pet. I want the pigeons!"

"Louie, please. Just give it a try. That's all I'm asking."

"No, it's not all you're asking. If I don't like it, are we going to move back? Because if it's up to me, I can save you a lot of trouble."

"But it's so much nicer out there. Wait till you see it. And it's safe. You'll have a lot more freedom out there. We won't have to worry about you so much all the time."

"Well, you can stop worrying about me. I'm perfectly safe, and I have all the freedom I want right here on the roof. You're just taking it away! How am I going to fly birds from out there, just tell me that."

"That's exactly the point, damn it!" Junior's voice was shaking.

"Junior, please," Ma pleaded. "Don't make it harder. Please."

"Well, I'll be damned if we worked our butts off to get her out of here and she goes around acting like we were committing a crime! The criminals are the ones who killed her friend, not us!"

I turned on him. "Don't you dare talk about Hector!" I cried. "It's all your fault. You want to move just to keep me off the roof. You can't stand it because I like it better up there than in this house. It's true! Casey's more my father than you'll ever be and he won't let you do this. You'll see. I'll go live with him if I have to, but I'm not moving out to Islip and I'm not leaving the roof and I hate your guts!"

For only the second time in my life, my mother smacked me across the face. I shut up immediately, but not because of the blow. I was more stunned by my own words. I had just said them, without thinking, but suddenly they offered the perfect solution: I would go live with Casey. I'd stay in Brooklyn and go out on Sundays to visit. How often did I see Ma and Frankie anyway? I was practically living on the roof. The solution was so simple I wondered why I hadn't thought of it before.

Later that night, I knocked on Frankie's door. He was sitting at his desk with his head in his hands. He hadn't said a word during the earlier conversation, and I had been trying to figure out why. He couldn't want to move any more than I did. What would he do without Michael? Without the Y?

"Frankie?"

He half-raised his head.

"You knew they were looking at a house, didn't you?"

After a pause, he nodded.

"You knew they were moving?"

"We're all moving, Louie."

"Why didn't you tell me?"

"Ma asked me not to. She said you'd get too upset."

"Aren't you upset?"

He shrugged. "What good would it do? Ma wanted to do this for a long time. Junior's giving up the store and everything. Try not to make it harder for them, okay?"

I could tell by the way he said it that he wasn't really on their side, but he wasn't on my side anymore either. For different reasons, I felt sorry for us both.

27

ONLY A YEAR BEFORE I WOULD HAVE THOUGHT THE sky was empty. Now, from the moment I left my house until I reached the corner of Bedford and North Eighth, I was alert. Something was out there. I could feel it. I searched the skies for it, knowing that any minute the microscopic figure of a bird would appear, winging its way out of the distance, either lost or heading for home. Before I knew it, I was standing on the sidewalk in front of Reliable Fabricators, touching the building with both hands. I ran my palms over the rough, red bricks, and a dusting of clay came off on my fingers.

I blinked and looked around. The doughnut shop was still across the street, the green station wagon was still parked on the corner. The edge of the coop was still visible from the sidewalk, and a line of pigeons was perched on top of it, silhouetted against the sky. I began the long climb to the roof.

By the time I reached the seventh floor, my hands were

shaking. I stood half-hidden in the doorway, trying to calm down. Casey was bent over inside the screen, examining a bird. Everything appeared sharper than usual, as if a slightly out-of-focus lens had finally been properly adjusted. The morning sun streamed in from the far side of the coop. Casey was absorbed in the stray and didn't notice me. After a minute, he stepped out of the screen to get a better look. When he pulled at the bird's leg, I could see the bands from across the roof: they were blue-and-white, one of Angelo's. Angelo had been losing babies to us all summer, but summer was over now and his birds should have learned how to get home. The carrier was just outside the shanty. Casey tossed the bird inside and shut the lid. Then he did a strange thing. Instead of heading back to the coop or chasing up the birds, he just stood there for a moment, his hands hanging empty at his side. And it occurred to me for the first time that once I was gone, Casey would be by himself again on the roof. He, too, would be alone.

"Casey!" I cried out. For a second I met his startled gaze, then I rushed across the roof into his arms. "Help me, Casey! Please! They're moving to the Island and they say I have to go. Don't let them take me, Casey. Please don't make me go!"

I tried to burrow my head into his stomach, but he grabbed my shoulders and pushed me a half step back.

"Whoa, whoa, wait a minute. What's going on here? Where'd you come from?" I grabbed his belt and wouldn't let go. "Stop that, Louie, what's the matter with you? Cut it out."

I fought the pressure of his hand under my chin.

"Talk to me. What the hell's the matter here?"

"I'm not going, Casey! I don't care what anybody says. It's not fair. They didn't even ask me. No one ever asks me anything. Please don't let them take me, Casey. If you let me stay with you I swear I'll do anything you want, I swear it, Case. I'll be so good you won't even know I'm there. If you tell them how much you need me for the roof and everything, and that you can't afford to let me go, maybe they'll listen to you. Please try, Casey. If I have to go out there I'll kill myself, I swear. I'll go crazy. I can't live without the birds."

"Slow down, baby. Just take it easy. You want a drink of water?"

I shook my head.

"Come over here."

He put his arm around my shoulders and led me over to the steps of the coop. I stumbled along beside him, still clutching his belt with one hand. I was afraid to let go. I was afraid he would disappear.

"Now come on, talk to me. Tell me what's going on here." He pulled me down next to him. I buried my face in his lap, and the tears poured out. I was crying, coughing, choking—I didn't care anymore. Casey pleaded with me to stop. He stroked my hair, he rocked me by the shoulders, but I couldn't help it. I cried so hard I left a snotty wet patch against his jeans. Gradually, the sobbing eased into short, ragged sniffles. I sat up and blew my nose on my sleeve.

"Hey. Don't do that." Casey reached into his back pocket and handed me a wrinkled handkerchief.

I brought it up to my face. It was still warm from his pocket, and it had the same yeasty smell as the coops. I burst into tears all over again.

"Jesus Christ, baby, take it easy! You're gonna make yourself sick." Casey patted my head over and over. "Please, baby, take it easy. Calm down. Just calm down. It ain't the end of the world." He rested his hand over the back of my neck. "I know how you feel, Louie. Shit. I cried for three days when I had to sell my first stock of pigeons. Three days! But I survived, you know what I mean? It's just pigeons."

After a while, I looked up. My nose was stuffy, and when I tried to speak the air backed up inside my head. "You cried?"

"Sure, I cried. Come on. That was my first stock of birds. I loved them, Louie. I'd had them up there maybe two, two and a half years. My old man made me get rid of them 'cause the neighbors complained, he didn't like that. But like I said, you get over it. It's not the end of the world."

I nestled under his arm and he pulled me close, letting me rest my cheek against his chest. He folded his arm around me, taking my hand in his, his thumb covering my fingers. His body formed a shield around me, and I wanted him never to let go.

Behind us, in the screen, the pigeons fluttered back and forth, clucking and gurgling, wondering what all the excitement was about. Those that had been out flying were now sunning themselves on top of the coop; the rest were scrounging for leftover grit or bathing in the metal trough. The pigeons had no tune, no song, but their soft, slurred murmur had a thousand variations. To me, it was still music.

Maybe it was because of my own outburst, but as we sat there listening to the birds, I realized for the first time in my life that animals never cried. They whimpered or howled if they were injured, but that was an automatic response: the involuntary whelp of pain. They possessed no such thing as tears. They never cried because they felt sorry for themselves, because life was unfair, because they wanted something they could never have.

Casey leaned back and started loosening his hold, but I

clutched on to his thumb. He bounced my hand against his knee. Little by little my breathing returned to normal.

"You think you can talk to me now? You wanna tell me what's going on, what this is all about?"

"They bought a house in Islip." I looked up into his face, hoping to find an answer, but he looked puzzled. "Case, they're moving to Long Island! Junior bought a house. I'm not going and I don't care what anybody says."

"Baby, what's the matter with you? It's beautiful out there. You'll have a yard and everything."

"Casey, you don't understand. What about the birds? I won't be able to fly the birds."

"Louie, what're you talking about? This move'll be good for you. They got better schools out there, it's cleaner. I wish I could buy a house out there. My kids were way better off when we lived on the Island than they are now. I mean it. That's one of the worst things I did for them, moving back here."

"When did you live on the Island? I thought you grew up here."

"I did. That was a long time ago. We moved out there just after the twins was born. We needed the room and my old lady couldn't stand Brooklyn. It was nice. We moved out by Patchogue."

"But what about the birds, Case? Did you have birds out there?"

"Nah. Are you kidding? It's a different kind of neighborhood out there. There ain't no pigeon-flyers. It's all single family homes, nice houses and everything."

"But didn't you miss the birds?"

"Nah, not exactly. I mean, I used to go up to other guys' roofs over here, hang around. I didn't really have no time for the sport. I had to drive over an hour to get to work, sometimes two. That used to drive me crazy, the commute. That's why we moved back. And then the payments were pretty steep, and my old lady had to go to work, and she had to start coming in every morning, and it just got to be too much."

"How long were you out there altogether?"

Case looked away. "Not even a year. Can you believe it? Nicest place I ever lived in my whole life and we didn't even last a year."

"But then you got to fly the birds again, right? After you moved back?"

"Oh, yeah. I had a lotta roofs since then."

"But didn't that make up for it? I mean, for moving back?"

"Didn't what make up for it?"

"The birds. Didn't that make it worthwhile?"

"Yeah. Sure." He was silent a minute. "My kids hated coming back here, especially the older ones. They started having trouble in school, they was always getting into things, and the little guy—he must of been about seven or eight—there was a gang a kids that had it in for him right from the start, used to beat the shit out of him every day after school. I hadda go around to every one of their houses. It was lousy. My wife hated coming back. We ain't never got along since then either, and that's the truth. Things was never the same."

"But don't they know how much the birds mean to you?"

"Louie, I'm telling you for the millionth time, there's more to life than flying pigeons. You don't wanna end up being a bum, you know what I mean?" He looked at me. "This here's no life for anybody, especially a girl. Your parents are right to get you out of here."

"Casey, how can you say that? What's wrong with flying the

birds? All of a sudden there's something wrong. I don't understand. You said I was the best chaser you ever had. Ever! Didn't you tell me that? That it had nothing to do with being a girl or not, I was just good with the birds? Casey, you know how much I love it here. Why are you telling me to leave?"

"Now, wait a minute. You're twisting everything I said."

"No, I'm not. I want to stay here, Casey. That's all. I want to stay and fly the birds. Don't you want me anymore?"

"Sure I do, baby. But you got an opportunity to get out of this here neighborhood, and to tell you the truth, I wish I could do the same thing for my kids. Your parents is only looking out for you, that's what you don't understand."

"How? By ruining my life?"

"Louie, maybe you don't always know what's best for you."

"Well, I know this, Casey. I love the birds. I don't want to leave. Everything just seems right up here, don't you know what I mean?"

Case stood up and rubbed his hands against his jeans. "Yeah. I know what you mean. But this ain't the real world, baby. This here's just a game." He jerked his head in the direction of the street. "You gotta have some kind of life down there." He walked over to the edge of the roof and stood there for a long time, looking down.

After what seemed like an eternity, I unwound myself from the steps and walked over next to him, close enough so that my shoulder brushed up against his forearm. I didn't look at him, but half-consciously mimicked his stance, as I had done a thousand times before. Below us, Brooklyn stretched out as far as the eye could see.

Casey shifted his weight and sighed. He put his hand over mine on the wall.

"Louie, you don't wanna end up like me. I know you like it up here, and you were a good flyer." The word "were" struck me like a fist in the stomach. "But this ain't no place for you. It ain't no place for me either." He tried to laugh.

"How can you say that? You love the game."

"I know, baby, but you gotta understand something. There's more to life than flying birds. This here sport traps you in a way. You get addicted, you can't let go. It sort of gets in the blood. You get hooked. You don't go away anywhere, you start cutting out of work, you neglect the family, you cut back on the social life. Little by little it becomes your whole world. You start running away up here when things is going wrong down there. That's okay sometimes, that's good, but after a while you don't never wanna hassle it out down there no more, you wanna run up to the roof. Pretty soon, you're up here all the time. And then one day you wake up and you got nothing left down there."

"But, Casey, you've got lots of friends." As soon as I said it, I was ashamed. Casey understood immediately.

"Don't worry about it. Them guys is all geeps anyway," he said bitterly. "Not that I give a shit. Don't misunderstand me. I don't care what any of them think, they're a bunch of mutts. But I never really got close to them, Louie. I ain't hardly got close to nobody my whole life, not really. Maybe it's better that way. I don't know. Even with the birds. It's just a hobby, you know. Just a game. That's why I said, if you gotta give it up, it's no big deal. They're just birds, Louie. It ain't nothing to get worked up about. You get too worked up over everything. You get too emotional. Things don't matter that much." He paused. "You understand what I'm saying? It's like with the birds. You remember what I told you? 'You catch, you lose;

you lose, you catch.' That's the name of the game. You don't want to be a mutt, do you?"

"But that's different, Case. I never held back up here, never. Only I'm not talking about one bird anymore. I'm talking about *everything*. If I have to move, I'll lose everything. And anyway, I don't belong out there. This is my home."

"Don't talk like that. You'll start school out there and make new friends. I bet you're gonna like it. You'll forget all about us back here, you'll see."

"Casey! I won't forget anything. How can you even say that?" He didn't answer. I lowered my voice. "I thought you'd want me to stay."

"Sure, I'd like you to stay. Of course I would. But you're gonna move and that's that. Facts of life, sweetheart. When your parents move, you gotta go with them. Right?"

I didn't answer.

"Am I right or wrong?"

I took a few deep breaths. Nothing was working out the way I'd planned. "But, Case, what about my idea?"

"What idea?"

"You know." I glanced up at him. He was looking out towards the river. "That I could come live with you."

He was silent for such a long time that I finally touched his arm. "Case?"

"Yeah, baby?"

"Did you hear me?"

He nodded slowly.

"Well?"

"Louie." He turned to look at me, started to say something, then changed his mind and just shook his head back and forth. "Louie, how old are you?"

"I'm almost eleven. Why?"

"Sweetheart, you don't—I've got five kids home, Louie. You got any idea what kind of zoo I live in? And even if I could take you home, your parents would never let you live with me. It'd be illegal or something."

"But what if Junior gave you money every month? I don't need much room, at home I don't even hardly have a room anyway. All I need is a bed. I could even sleep on the floor, really I could. Frankie and me used to sleep on the floor all the time when we were little, we pretended we were cowboys sleeping on the trail. Really, Case, it doesn't even bother me. And I'll stop eating so much, I promise. I'll work for Joey and start paying for more things up on the roof. I'll do anything you say, I promise. I'll be good, Casey. I'll be perfect. Just don't let them take me away."

"Louie, baby, I'm sorry. That's your family. You gotta go with them, I can't do nothing."

"But I want to stay with you!" I pushed closer to him, pressing against his side until he had to look at me. His eyes were very bright, bluer than I had ever seen them.

"I know you do, sweetheart. But that's another chapter." Neither one of us said anything for a long time. When Casey broke the silence, I knew that I had lost. "You're still a kid, Louie. You'll get over it. Now you got to do what your parents tell you to do. They're moving to the Island for you and your brother. I'm telling you, it's a lot nicer out there. You'll see. You won't wanna come back."

"Casey, I want to fly the birds. I can't do that if I move out there."

"Sure you can. You can come in on the weekends. Come up on the roof anytime. You're always welcome. You know that.

How's that sound? You'll probably be so busy with your new friends you won't even want to come back."

"And how am I supposed to get here? Walk?"

"Nah. Somebody'll bring you in."

"Yeah? Like who?" My eyes were glistening with tears, but my voice had become flinty and hard-edged.

"I don't know. Your father'll bring you in. He'll come back on business, don't you think?"

"He's not my father. I've told you that a million times."

" 'Scuse me. Your *step*father."

"You know he won't bring me in. It's his fault we're moving in the first place. He hates the birds and he hates me. Which is okay because I hate him, too."

"You do not hate him. Cut it out."

"I do too, Casey! Don't tell me I don't hate him! What do you know? He's the one who talked my mother into wanting to move. Otherwise she would never have gone out there. Anyway, what's that got to do with who's gonna drive me back to fly the birds? Huh, Case? Are you gonna do it? You want to pick me up every weekend?" For a moment I hated him too, because I knew the answer. Casey wouldn't come for me, he wouldn't do anything that required time or money or effort or responsibility. He had just said nothing was worth it. I'd only asked him out of spite, to make him feel bad.

"Yeah." He sounded insulted. "Maybe I will. Maybe I'll just do that."

"Sure." I glared at him.

"I mean that. If you want to come in so bad, I'll come and get you. I can do that."

I didn't move a muscle. In the distance, traffic boomed on the B.Q.E.

"Louie." I fastened my eyes on the rooftops and tried to blot out his voice. "Louie, I didn't mean to hurt your feelings. I was just trying to cheer you up." He paused and took a deep breath. "You wouldn't want to live with me anyway. It's a circus, baby, I ain't kidding. Sometimes I don't even wanna go back there myself. I know I ain't supposed to say that, but it's true. Louie, there's things—there's things I can't say to nobody. I don't—I mean, I can't—" He shook his head. "I wish—" He broke off and started pacing back and forth. There was a knot of pain burning at the back of my throat. "Louie, this may be hard for you to understand. I don't always do the right thing. You know that, right?" I flashed my angriest look at him, but he had turned away and was watching the sky. "I liked having you up here. You're a good kid. You were almost like a partner. I mean that. I don't want you to go away, it's a tough break, but that's the way it goes. You'll be glad later on. Like I said, I wished I coulda done it for my kids."

There was an empty wine bottle tilted against the trash can. Case bent down, picked it up, and walked back over beside me. He dangled the bottle over the edge of the roof for several seconds, then let go. I watched it fall seven stories and smash against the sidewalk, all in slow motion. Nothing seemed real anymore.

"Louie, I promise I'll come pick you up, okay? Just write down your address and everything and I'll come out and get you. You'll see." He wiped his forehead on his sleeve. "There ain't much happening up here during the week anyway, you know that. The action's really Saturday, Sunday, so you ain't gonna miss nothing. It ain't like you're really gonna miss anything."

But I knew it was a lie. I would miss everything. I would

walk off the roof and out into the street, and everything I cared about would be gone. I knew it, and suddenly I realized that Casey knew it too. The difference was, Casey couldn't admit the loss. On the roof, with the birds—yes. But not for me. That was different. And certainly not for himself. Casey had no more room for losses. There was already too much missing from his life.

I looked all around me. I could see hundreds of rooftops, many still dotted with coops. If Casey were right, someday this would all be gone. Little by little the pigeon game was starting to disappear. Someday it would die out completely. The last old-timer would pass away and the last pigeon would be removed from the last roof. And what would happen then? Would anyone remember that once there had been two worlds here, that life had not always begun and ended on the street?

I could feel Casey standing next to me. I would remember, I was sure of that. No matter where I lived or how old I got, I had only to look up to know that there was something more. Everything else in the world might change, but the skies would always be alive.

Casey had given this to me. He had been a good teacher. Better than he knew.

He reached over and stroked my hair, then tilted my chin so I had to face him. "I promise I'll come get you, baby. You don't gotta say good-bye to nothing, understand? You ain't gotta give up nothing. We're a team, all right? We'll always be a team. I'll come out there every weekend and pick you up. You'll go right on flying the birds with me, just like always, okay? That's a promise, Louie. I swear to god."

I wanted to look at him—I knew I would never see him again—but my eyes burned with tears and I had to look away.

215

"Don't do that, sweetheart. Please, baby. Don't be sad. Believe me, nothing's gonna change between us, I'm telling you. I swear to god, nothing's gonna change."

As we stood there, something spooked the birds and they spiraled out against the sky.

I couldn't move. I couldn't speak.

Casey knelt down beside me. "What's the matter, Louie? Tell me. Please. Don't you believe me?"

It took a long time to steady my voice. "Sure I do, Casey. Honest." I reached over and touched his face. "I believe you."